# QUIET

## ON THE PORCH

JOCELYN M. LEE

ISBN: 979-8-218-75193-7 (Paperback)



Website: msjocelynlee.com

Instagram: @jocelynmleeauthor

Facebook: https://www.facebook.com/drjleethegrowthcoach

Email: info@jocelynmlee.com

Pen Your Point Communications, LLC

Published, December 2025

*In memory of my father, John Nolan*

*Dedicated to my mother, Ethel Nolan, and my Ohio
tribe*

# Books

by Jocelyn M. Lee

Non-Fiction

Stop Hiding: Unlock Your Full Potential and Embrace the
Five Pillars of a Growth Mindset

Hush A Minute: The Companion Coach to Stop Hiding

# AUTHOR'S NOTE

This novel unfolds through multiple perspectives, providing a layered and intimate view of a reimagined Oakwood in Montgomery County, Dayton, Ohio, and the lives that intersect on and around the Goodman family porch.

Janelle – The daughter raised in love, navigating truth, identity, and becoming.

Justice – A man driven by legacy, living with purpose, poured love into every nail but couldn't fix what cracked beneath the surface.

Olive – A keeper of silence and strength, who refused to surrender to what tried to undo her. She stood anyway. Loved anyway. Built anyway.

The Porch – A witness to everything, balancing laughter and grief, secrets and silence with equal grace.

Each chapter signals its narrator by tone and memory, guiding you through the tangled lives of a family bound by more than blood.

*Love is the softer of sorrow,*

*the assuager of grief,*

*the mother of happiness*

*-unknown*

# TABLE OF CONTENTS

# PART ONE

*And the porch, for all its silence, listened like an old friend.*

# ONE

# QUIET ON THE PORCH

June 18, 2003-1:00 p.m.

Dayton, Ohio

Oakwood, Montgomery County

OLIVE GOODMAN STOPPED the truck in the middle of Liberty Lane and cried. Not because she had run out of fuel—her husband, Justice, always kept the tank full. Not because of a dirty cab—the vintage D100 was pristine, shining with bright yellow paint, chrome polished to a mirror finish. Not because children playing in the street blocked her way—no children, no traffic. Yet the tears rolled down her cheeks onto her aged, freckled hands, like drizzle on toffee candy. She cried because her tears were the only place for grief to go. Heartbreak consumed her, blurring the lines between what had been and what still felt real.

She sat motionless in her husband's truck; her body molded to the leather seat. The air inside still smelled of him. She breathed in deeply, pine, Old Spice, and the warm trace of something that always felt like home. Her fingers curled tighter around the steering wheel; his presence felt as if she were sitting beside him.

The neighborhood was unnaturally quiet, no sounds of children's laughter, no echoes of barking dogs, no rhythms of rumbling bass from the car down the street. A red tricycle lay tipped on its side in the neighbor's yard. A basketball sat abandoned in the gutter. The stillness weighed her down like rain on a drenched cloth; perhaps Oakwood knew. Olive, a wife who had just become a widow, was keenly aware of how quickly news traveled in this tight-knit community.

She turned the truck into the long, familiar driveway, flanked by lilies on one side and burning bush on the other. On the left sat his house, blue shutters drawn, its quiet presence holding steady like an exhale. On the right, her cottage, the one Justice built with calloused hands and humble pride, not just to win her back, but to prove he'd changed. It was the house she returned to, not because he pleaded, but because that time, she knew he meant it.

She gazed out at the stretch of land behind the two homes,

and the memory came rushing back, the day he shared his dream with her. The sun had wrapped itself around them like approval, and the fields shimmered with promise, even though, truth be told, they were overgrown, uneven, and nowhere near ready. But somehow, through his eyes, even the mess looked like a future.

Justice Goodman returned from the Korean War with a purpose, the GI Bill, and a share of his parents' estate. He cleared the road through farmland and dedicated himself to creating something lasting. The houses, the barn, they were all built by his hands. A community for veterans, a place where gardens grew and causes found champions. Where oak trees and children were protected and could play in peace.

Olive held the memory like breath held underwater. Justice had pulled his pick-up truck up to the land they'd now claimed as home, the heat rising in waves off the road. He had jumped out, circled to her side, and opened the door with a crooked grin. "I'll make us a life we can both live in," he had said.

Her reminiscence persisted, overriding her trance-like posture, as if motion could undo her. She reached across the bench and picked up his gloves, the cowhide worn soft to his grip. In that moment, she closed her eyes and submitted to the restless reflection, before it all began, an evening visit to his parents' home, Horace Sr. and Bea Goodman.

Back then, Ma Bea was already a widow, and Olive found herself sitting in her parlor, perched on the bristled settee that still carried traces of the man who once ruled the room. The house buzzed with chatter, the clatter of utensils, and blue notes. Olive didn't know it then, not fully, but that moment, in that chair, in that house, was the beginning of everything that came next.

# TWO

# A RING DON'T BUILD NOTHING

THE ROOFTOPS OF the Haymarket District melted into soft silhouettes beneath an amber sky. Crickets struck up a quiet chorus, their song mingling with the flicker of fireflies that stitched the dusk with movement.

From the wide picture window of his parents' home, Olive watched Justice on the porch swing, one leg tucked under him, the other swinging easy, like he used to when he was just a boy beside his father. His body leaned hard into the curve of the swing, and the furrows on his brow told her everything. She knew the Oakwood land deal was pressing on him. Red had said it would be settled tonight, but Olive understood her man, Justice didn't rest easy unless he was holding all the pieces. And right now, they weren't fitting together.

Horace Goodman Sr. had built a life from sawdust and sweat. Farmer, store owner, and general contractor, self-taught, self-made. He passed the businesses on to his sons, focusing on the parts that matched their strengths, the way he knew, and they didn't, so he taught them. He handed them a blueprint not just for work, but for how to stand up in the world.

Justice was grounded in his father's philosophies, and he quoted them often to Olive. "Hard work never killed nobody. Don't squander your money. Love your wife. Be good to her. Family first, after the good Lord. And stay away from the poison." Hard work didn't kill his father. Liquor was the very poison Horace Sr. warned Justice about, and yet somehow passed on anyway.

Olive's eyes followed Justice as he rose, rubbed the weariness from his face, and stepped through the front door of his parents' home. The air inside greeted them like a family cookout, thick with the smell of skillet cornbread and fried pork chops, rich and familiar. The house vibrated with life. Ma Bea corralling grandbabies like a seasoned conductor, pots banging their rhythm in the kitchen, and the sultry swing of Ellington and Coltrane threading through from a back room. The moment Justice crossed the threshold, something in him loosened, and when it did, Olive felt herself soften too.

Clyde, the oldest, reclined in their daddy's easy chair like a man born to it. With his sharp jawline and lazy grin, he could've passed for Caesar Romero, if someone swapped his flannel shirt and steel-toe boots for a tuxedo. Across from him, his wife, Sheryl, flipped through *Life* magazine, unbothered by the whirlwind of their children. Regal even in a house dress, she looked like Dorothy Dandridge waiting on her cue, just trade the cotton frock for a ball gown and she'd be red-carpet ready.

Justice stepped into the room with a grin that lit up the space. "Hey, family!" he called, arms wide like he was gathering the whole house into a hug.

The kids rushed him, latching onto his legs like vines on a trellis. "Uncle Justice! Are you buying a farm? Can we live with you?"

"Sketch. Lena. Twins, go sit down somewhere," Sheryl snapped, flipping through the magazine without looking up.

Justice chuckled, nudging the kids gently. "Alright, ankle-biters. Do what your mama says."

Lena, undeterred, beamed up at him with her gap-toothed smile. "Uncle Jus, can we pleeeease?"

"I'll have to check with my wife," he said, dragging the word out with a sly grin. "My wife," he added, repeating it under his breath like he was trying it on for size.

Across the room, Olive lifted her hand and wiggled her naked ring finger. "Wife?" she said, squinting playfully. "You see a ring, Justice Goodman?"

Justice leaned back, full of theater. "A ring?" he said. "A ring don't plant no crops. It can't fix a fence or milk a cow. It don't build a dream or stretch across acres. It don't raise livestock, or…"

Olive stepped in close and bumped his shoulder, cutting him off with a look. "Who you rehearsing that speech for?" she asked, calm and sure. "Because it's not for me. I've known the dream from the beginning. I'm here for it, ten toes down. You must be practicing for some other woman who hasn't already got a line on the deed for her signature."

Justice blinked, startled by the hint of truth in her tone.

Then Olive broke into a laugh, low, and familiar, like the kind that sneaks up when love runs deep and history sits close.

Across the room, Sheryl wagged a finger. "Yes, you need a ring. Doesn't have to be big. You can always upgrade. I did; every baby came with a bigger diamond." She held up her hand, flashing an emerald-cut diamond that practically applauded itself.

Clyde chuckled. "Every single one," he said. "We've got the receipts."

Olive rested a hand on Justice's back, rubbing slow circles like she was drawing him into himself. She looked into those espresso-dark eyes, still boyish, still full of heart. She saw something more than affection there—something awake.

"I already upgraded," she whispered, and kissed him on the cheek.

Justice's grin stretched wide. "Wait… did you just propose to me?"

Olive's eyes danced. "Maybe."

She turned to Lena, who had been hanging on every word. "And 'wife,'" she called out, "means y'all can stay with us anytime you want."

"Even all summer?" Lena squealed.

"Even then," Olive said, sliding her hand into Justice's.

He gave it a gentle squeeze, chuckling. "Well then, I better get to work on that fence… and the ring."

Horace Jr., two years younger than Clyde but nearly his twin in build, walked out from the back bedroom with chestnut-hued skin and silver starting to show through his hairline. He was dressed like it was Sunday morning, waxed suede loafers, showing off their velvety texture, slacks creased sharp enough to slice air, and a teal shirt pressed so perfectly it looked poured onto his chest. His mustache was shaped with surgical precision, and the smile he flashed, half Gable, half game, landed on Justice like a dare. "Hey, boy," he said, voice smooth as a warning. "So, how much do you need?"

Justice glared at his brother, those strong Goodman genes ran deep; hair so thick and wavy, it couldn't keep a side part, sharp features that hinted at Native roots, though by the time he came along, it seemed his older brothers had hijacked most of the melanin. He had fair skin, and when irritated, it showed, his face flushed quickly and hot. A tell he never could hide. At

Horace Jr.'s question, the red crept up his neck like a warning flare. He didn't answer. Instead, Olive caught the shift in his posture, eyes sweeping the room, jaw tightening, searching for Red.

She recognized the pattern; Justice didn't like being cornered, especially by blood. He needed space to think, to calculate. She reached down and smoothed the cuffs of her pedal pushers, a small, steadying act, one she always did when the room got too tight for him. The silence held just long enough to singe, and then Ma Bea entered, breaking it with the scent of lilies, orange blossom, and something fried.

Ma Bea navigated the room like royalty, wearing a crown of silver curls with their own attitude, apron tight around her middle. She met Justice in the middle of the large parlor and handed her son an envelope with fingers trembling slightly. "Your father's Farmer's Life policy been good to us," she said. Reading the tension, she leaned in and whispered in her son's ear. "Red didn't tell them about your land deal, baby. These Goodmans are just nosy. Junior eavesdropped on me and Red earlier."

"Where is Red?" Justice asked.

"Went to pick up Cayenne. He'll be back." In the meantime, she surveyed the room, taking her baby boy by the hand, eyes warm, voice resolute, she addressed her children. "I've got a policy I haven't cashed in." She winked. "It is signed that the beneficiary is Beatrice Goodman, in case anyone is wondering. I plan to give it to Justice for the Oakwood property. Your daddy would approve."

Justice's throat tightened. "Momma."

In her momma don't play voice, she said. "Now, go build something."

She kissed his forehead, proud and firm. She turned her head, and her eyes met her oldest son. "Clyde, once your brother has what he needs, y'all split the rest."

"Yes, ma'am," Clyde replied, calm as ever. Olive didn't miss the ease in his tone. Clyde had been set for years, firstborn, first to get trained by their father, to turn a profit. He didn't need the money. He'd had a jumpstart while Justice was still laying the foundation.

Red swept through the doorway with Cayenne on his heels, perfume first, attitude close behind. She strutted in like she owned the place, eyes sharp and smile loaded. "Mmm-hmm… is that cabbage I smell? And fried okra? Don't mess with me now, Ma Bea, what's on that stove?" She didn't wait for an answer. "I brought my mac n' cheese, just in case you needed a little extra love. You know Red l-u-u-v-e-s it." Her words rolled out like gospel with a twist, and before anyone could blink, she was halfway to the kitchen, nose lifted like a Sunday bloodhound sniffing out a blessing. Ma Bea wrinkled her nose but managed a patient smile.

Justice marched toward Red, clenched jaw, holding the insurance policy in his hand, but Red pulled him into a bear hug before he could speak. "See, man? Told you I got you. Now let's eat."

***

When Olive stepped out of the truck, her knees buckled. She didn't know which direction to walk. His house? Hers? Both held pieces of him. She chose the porch, their shared sanctuary. The place that remembered everything. Where her daughter's laughter once echoed, where neighbors stopped to gossip, to plan, to breathe.

Inside the house, the scent of cedarwood, aftershave, and something warm hit her like a wall. His glasses case lay on the coffee table. His Cubs cap hung on the hook she always said was too low. A newspaper sat neatly folded. And there was one sealed envelope addressed to their daughter. She didn't touch it. Just sat in his recliner.

It was quiet on the porch. The stillness wasn't peaceful. It was the kind that followed finality. The kind that pressed down until all that remained were tears. Overwhelmed by his presence inside the stately walls and unable to lay hold of him, she stepped back onto the porch and sat on the repurposed truck bench. Her hands gripped the armrests as if they were the only things anchoring her.

She stared into the dusk and whispered, "Lord, give me the words. Our daughter is coming home." Not for a wedding. Not for flowers or vows. But for a folded flag, an obituary, and something else. Something she had buried so long ago it had started to rise again like smoke from the edges of memory.

# THREE

# HEAT RISES

June 17, 2003

THE MOONLIGHT WAS wide, lying across the yard like a soft sheet. Justice Goodman disliked nights like this, when the air sagged heavy and hot, sticking to him like grief. He had witnessed how hot nights always had a way of leaving hurt behind by morning. Sleep fled from him on nights like this one. Memories rushed in, poignant and sharp, seeping through the heat.

PTSD launched a stealthy attack, and images flashed before him— the night the command post fell near Pork Chop, the sky crackling with gunfire, the earth shaking under his boots. Heat rose everywhere. Big Rob had been trapped first, pinned beneath two broken beams, blood pooling beneath him faster than either of them could think. Justice clawed at the wreckage, hands raw, shoulders burning, cursing under his breath. Rob, calm even in dying, ordered him away. "Quit now, soldier. It's done." But Justice wouldn't quit. He stayed, gritting his teeth, fighting wood, fire, and fate, until the sun rose slow and mean over the horizon. When the light came, the truth followed. Big Rob was gone. It was hot then. It is hot now. And every drop of sweat on Justice's skin carried a memory he couldn't outrun.

In a pair of old gray slacks and a white T-shirt that had thinned with time, he sat alone on the porch, the repurposed bench seat from an old Chevy creaking beneath him, his old bones groaning just as loudly. The same porch where his daughter once had lounged beside him, her head on his shoulder when she first told him about the man she loved, Red's boy. He had smiled then, or something that passed for a smile. A crooked version, the kind that said, No one is good enough for my baby, even if it is a boy who carries my brother's name.

The unspoken had sat on his chest for years, a quiet weight that never shifted, no matter how tightly he pressed it down. He'd followed instructions, his brother Red's instructions, at the adoption agency that day, standing awkward and neatly dressed while the baby lay swaddled in a rose-colored blanket, soft and still and already claimed by Olive's heart. "No questions," Red had said. "That's how this stays clean."

Justice had wanted to ask everything. Who's the father? Where's the mother? Why us? Why me and Olive? But Red's jaw was locked, and the social worker avoided his eyes like a guilty priest.

By the time he turned to Olive, she had already cradled the child against her chest. "God sent her," she'd whispered. And just like that, no queries were required. But Justice had never stopped wondering. Now she had grown. In love. Ready to step into a new life. And he couldn't let her walk into a future without the truth.

He closed his eyes and tilted his head back, letting the air settle around him like judgment. The cicadas were loud. The fan inside the screen door clicked as it turned, cutting the silence just enough to remind him he wasn't fully alone, not yet. He had rehearsed it alone in the mirror, repeating the words now as if they might soften the reveal if he could say them right.

"You were born in secret, baby girl," his voice reverent and rough, "but you are not a mistake." He imagined cupping her face gently, as if she might break under the weight of it all if he wasn't careful. "You were the answer," he whispered. "An answer to your mama's prayer long before she ever knew your name. She asked God for a child to love, and He sent you. Not how she expected or dreamed when she was young, depositing her dreams in pitcher plants." He smiled, sad and proud all at once. "You didn't come easy, and you didn't come clean. But you came right on time."

Whenever he imagined the words leaving his mouth, they caught somewhere between his chest and throat. Olive had said it once, years ago. Some truths don't come in words. They come in what we do. And he'd believed that–then. But now he wasn't sure it was enough. He looked over at the cottage, the one he had built for Olive, close enough for love, distant enough for her dignity. It was a strange arrangement by most folks' standards, a husband and wife living side by side but not under the same roof. It worked for them.

Olive had never been the kind to trade freedom for appearances, and Justice had loved her too much to ask her to. He had heard that some of her friends, the honest ones anyway, had once confessed they envied her, that kind of peace, that kind of arrangement, where love didn't mean losing yourself.

The lights were off. She was in there somewhere, sleeping, or pretending to, resting in that stubborn faith she wrapped around herself like a second skin. She wore the scriptures like a breastplate, like the one she kept on her nightstand. "I lay down and slept, I woke again, for the Lord sustained me." Justice smiled faintly, hearing her voice in his mind, teasing him. "If God's awake, there's no need for me to be."

He thought about dialing up his daughter, Janelle, then, in the twilight. Thought about waking her to hear her voice one last time before everything cracked open. But he didn't. Instead, he remained on the worn truck seat, allowing the weight of it all to press down until the ribs in his back creaked and his bones ached- remnants of a decades-old automobile accident, driving while drunk and slamming into the metal guardrails near Lakeside Amusement Park. He whispered a prayer that didn't start with "Dear God" and didn't end with "Amen." It just hung there in the heat.

The dawn of June 18th crept in like a whisper. Justice pulled open the window above his bed, reaching up with both hands until the sash clicked into place. The breeze had been hiding all night. Now the sun was up, coaxing it out and softening the weight of the heat. He lay back on the bed, head tucked just beneath the open window, eyes closed. "When the breeze comes outta hiding, he muttered, I'm gon' catch tha son of a bitch and wring the air outta it!"

The room was quiet, still damp with the ghosts of his thoughts from the day before. Caesar, his gray muzzled German Shepherd, barked. Not the usual feed-me bark. Not the goofy, tail-wagging woof that meant the mailman had come and gone. This one was different, sharp, full of frustration, the kind of bark Caesar used when something wasn't right.

Justice's eyes snapped open. The dog's howl thundered deep and guttural through the high Victorian walls, echoing off the cabinets and floorboards like a warning bell. Footsteps? He wondered. He couldn't catch the rhythm, but Caesar knew the porch patterns, the old dog had grown wise to porch echoes— how joy walked lighter than grief, how shame barely touched the steps at all. He had sniffed out secrets long before they were spoken.

And this time, something in the air—an offbeat, unfamiliar weight. Caesar didn't bark again. He just stood, tail low, ears pointed toward the door, as if he already knew what was coming. Justice sat up slowly, swung his legs off the bed, and rubbed a hand over his face. "Easy now, boy," he muttered.

"Ain't no need for drama this early." Caesar didn't let up.

Justice stood, bones creaking under him like old porch wood. He moved toward the front of the house, noticing a slight tightness in his chest, not sharp, but enough to make him pause, just like it had before. He did what he always did, breathed through it, told himself it was nothing, and kept walking. Part of him already knew. Whatever was coming, it wasn't Olive's cooking for breakfast.

The knocking came sharply and erratically. Not polite. Not patient. Justice made his way to the door, Caesar pacing behind him like a sentry. The dog let out a low growl, then sat at his side, tense, watching. Justice opened the door fast, hand still on the knob when it swung out. The edge nearly caught her in the face.

Eva DuBois. She stood barefoot on the porch, one hand raised to knock again, the other clutching a brown paper sack. Her gray hair was wild, clinging to her damp forehead like forgotten thread. She reeked of last night's liquor and something sour. "Well, look who finally came to the damn door," she said, voice too loud for the morning.

Justice didn't move. Just stood there, jaw clenched.

Eva leaned in, grinning that devil's smile she wore when she knew she was getting under someone's skin. "I saw her. I saw baby girl on the news, you know. Little press princess. Fancy job, big office in Che-kaa-go, gonna marry a pretty boy with teeth too perfect to be honest."

"Eva, gon somewhere with your mess. Not today," Justice said, pacing and even.

"Not today? Not to-damn-day?" she shouted, jabbing a bony finger into his chest. "You think you get to pick the day, Goodman? You? And your holy brother?" Her voice cracked. The smirk faltered. "He said he loved me. Said I was light in his darkness. But he went back to that lace-gloved wife and left me with a baby I couldn't name. And you," her voice dropped into something rough and guttural, "you two just took her. Like she was a coat someone forgot at church."

Justice's hand tightened on the doorframe.

Eva's eyes sharpened, gleaming like broken glass. "And now she's gonna marry her damn brother, and no one's sayin' nothin.' Not Red, not his God, not even you." She stepped closer. "You gonna let that happen, soldier?"

Something dropped inside him. Hard. Sharp. Irrevocable. The words hit like gunfire, loud, final, and already too late to outrun. It reeled him back to the day he heard the doctor's words, "You've got damage."

It was the day he learned he couldn't father children. The doctor's words had been clinical, but their impact was like a detonation. He had nodded, pretended to understand, pretended it didn't gut him. Walked out into the blinding afternoon sun like a man trying not to fall apart in front of strangers. He had thought of Olive instantly. Of the dreams they'd envisioned in long conversations. The farmhouse, the laughter of children, and her eyes bright with motherhood. And now, this.

He remembered sitting alone in the truck, all those years ago, wondering how to tell her. How to say the one thing that might crack her open in the same way he now felt fractured. Back then, he'd waited. Waited days. Then weeks. As if the delay could somehow lessen the heartbreak.

# FOUR

# HOPE BLOOMS

THE DOCTOR DIDN'T look him in the eye. Just fiddled with the chart and tapped a pen on the folder before saying it, low and clinical. "You've got damage. From the war. Scarring. You may not be able to father children."

Justice nodded, but it wasn't agreement. It was armor. He stared at the door behind the doctor's shoulder, as if Olive might walk through it and make the moment disappear. But she didn't.

He walked to the truck alone. He'd carried the truth for weeks, turning it over in his mind, searching for the right words. Olive had been disappointed by life too many times, and he couldn't bear to be the one to add weight to that burden.

He waited for hope to show up. His daddy always told him, 'Hope is like your best man.' Hope that the right words might soften the blow. Hope that timing could cushion the truth. But the delay didn't ease the heartbreak. It only gave it more room to bloom.

The words didn't come easily. They sounded foreign coming from his mouth, "I can't," like something he'd never been taught to say. Olive didn't speak right away. Just took his hand, pressed it to her cheek, and held it there. He cried in silence, then swept the sorrow beneath sawdust and service. If he couldn't give Olive the dream, they'd held close, he'd build something bigger. A legacy. A community. Like his daddy before him. He'd make room for other folks' dreams, even if his own had slipped through his calloused hands.

The house was too quiet. So, they signed the papers to foster. He didn't expect to fall in love with the boy. Quiet. Brown-eyed. Left paper airplanes around the house and called Justice "sir" one day and "Dad" the next. That one stuck.

Then came the letter. The boy had been placed, "matched with a long-term home," they said. Justice held the page in one hand and the boy's airplane in the other. Olive sobbed in the next room. He didn't go to her. He just stood still, heart thudding, unable to look at the porch without seeing that boy waving goodbye.

Two weeks later, he brought home the adoption forms. "You sure?" Olive asked, voice soft.

Justice shrugged one shoulder. "*Or* we could just get a dog."

She blinked, caught off guard. "A dog?"

"Yeah," he said, a hint of a grin pulling at the corner of his mouth. "One that barks when he's happy and won't leave when things get hard."

Olive gave a small laugh, the first in days. "Well, if we're dreaming, I want the kind that can babysit."

He smiled fully then. "Fine. We'll get a baby and a dog. One for now, one for later."

She shook her head, wiping the corner of her eye. "You're a plumb fool."

"Yeah," he said. "But you're stuck with me." He didn't say anything more. Just opened the folder, laid out the paperwork, and started writing their names. They'd make room. For a child. For hope. For something that wouldn't leave.

***

But heartbreak, like truth, had no interest in convenience. And it was coming. Just like their daughter was coming home now. With questions. With a need to know everything he had tried and failed to protect her from.

*Red and Eva? Janelle. Gonna marry her brother? Julien? The baby in the rose-colored blanket. No questions, Red had said. No questions.*

But now, now he knew the one question he should've asked. He staggered back half a step. Not visibly, not in the way that would've given Eva power, but inside, his chest buckled, a new tightness wrapped around his ribs, hot and blooming.

His mind reached for something to ground him, Olive's voice, the porch swing's creak, the smell of beans on the stove. But nothing came. Not even a breath. He wanted to slam the door. He wanted to grab Eva and shake her, shake the poison out of her. But mostly, God help him, he wanted it not to be true.

Caesar barked again. Sharp. Jarring.

Eva turned and staggered off the porch, muttering curses and prophecies to the morning air. Then, halfway down the steps, she stopped. She danced. Not in rhythm. Not in joy. But in a slow, drifting way, elbows, wrists, sway. Something inside her had broken open and spilled out in movement instead of words. She twirled once in the gravel, barefoot, arms outstretched like broken wings, remembering how to fly. Then she slipped into her car, slammed the door, and pulled away in a cloud of dust and exhaust. Leaving silence thick enough to choke on.

Justice stood there long after she'd gone. The breeze had finally found its way inside, cool and soft against the back of his neck. But it didn't feel like peace. It felt like a warning. He didn't follow. He didn't close the door. He just stood in the doorway, Caesar growling low beside him, the last note of Eva's haunted dance infiltrating the atmosphere.

And now, everything he had built, his family, his home, his hope, was trembling beneath the weight of one unbearable truth. A dull ache bloomed beneath his ribs, familiar now, and unwelcome. He pressed a hand to the frame, steadying himself, willing it away. Not today, he thought, not like this.

His mind reeled, still catching up to what Eva had just hurled at him. Janelle. *His* Janelle. Red and Eva's baby? The pieces didn't make sense, didn't fit together, not yet. But the truth had cracked open something he couldn't put back. He hadn't even begun to process it, didn't have time to. Not with the weight pressing in from all sides, his chest, his conscience, the porch itself.

He reached for the phone and dialed Olive. He figured she would be right in the middle of rinsing the beans and setting them to boil in a pot. He knew she'd think it was a strange hour for a call, even stranger coming from him. But something in him knew he had to hear her voice, even if he didn't know what he was about to say. He dialed.

Olive picked up. "Mornin'."

"Wife," he said, his voice dense and measured.

She clutched her dish towel. "You, okay?" concern threaded her words.

"A little pressure in my chest. I'm heading to the VA to get checked out. Don't worry, I'll be fine. I probably strained somethin' out there foolin' with that barn."

"Want me to come with you?" Worry tinged her voice.

"No need. I'll call you once they check me out. We're having beans today, if I remember right?"

"Yes, they are cooking now." She said.

"I will be back before they come out of the pot." He placed the receiver back on the base, took a deep breath, and with one hand pressed to his chest, Justice climbed into the yellow truck and drove himself to the VA, like a man determined to wrestle time for just one more day.

# FIVE

# PUNCH LIST

OLIVE WAS POURING bacon grease into a pot of beans when the phone rang, one of those hollow landline chimes that seemed to travel through a tunnel. She wiped her hands on her apron and answered on the second ring as if she had been expecting it. "Hello. Justice?"

"Mrs. Goodman?" The voice pierced through the line.

"Yes, this is Olive Goodman."

"This is Dr. Amir Roy from the VA Medical Center. I've admitted Mr. Goodman. Your husband's condition has worsened in the last few hours, and I'm sorry to say, I don't have good news. I know this isn't the news you were expecting. You should come to the hospital right away."

"Oh Lord… Yes, I am on my way. Please tell my husband I am on my way!" She didn't ask any questions. She dropped the line and the ladle, turned off the fire, and tossed the lid on the pot before snatching her purse from the hook by the door and grabbing the keyring off the sunflower-shaped dish. Her breath caught in her throat as she rushed out the door. Her hands trembled as she slid into the driver's seat of the Buick.

A silver van sped into the driveway beside the Buick as Olive turned the key in the ignition. Cayenne jumped out of the driver's door, holding a glass loaf pan wrapped in a towel, steam curling around her fingers. "Olive?" she called, concern already rising in her chest. "Where you headed?"

Olive leaned out of the window, her face pale and drawn. "It's Justice. He's at the VA. His heart," She shook her head. "I don't know if he's going to make it."

Cayenne didn't hesitate. She shoved the bread pan wafting of crackling cornbread into Olive's lap and ran around the car, opening the driver's side door. "Scoot over. I'm driving." Olive held the warm dish like a lifeline.

The two women didn't talk much on the way to the VA. The air between them was tense with urgency. Cayenne gripped the steering wheel so tightly her knuckles turned pink. She pulled the car into the campus, and the two women got out and jogged to the patient entrance. Once inside the reception area, Olive announced, "I am here for Justice Goodman."

Inside the VA, the lighting was bright white and sterile. The lobby buzzed with controlled chaos, phones ringing, intercom calls, wheelchairs gliding across the vinyl tile. The scent of antiseptic clung to the air, mingling with the faint aroma of coffee from a nearby vending machine. The receptionist looked up at the sound of Olive's voice, but before she could speak, a young man in a light blue shirt beneath a navy hospital vest stepped forward.

"They're with him now, in CCU, room 312," he said gently. "I know Mr. Goodman; I saw him in the ER earlier today. He didn't look good. I stayed with him until they admitted him. I just came from upstairs checking on him." Almost as if he were standing at attention, the uniformed man glanced between Olive and Cayenne with quiet compassion. "Let me escort you, this way."

Olive and Cayenne moved like dancers through the hallways, one leading, one close behind. When they reached the room, they paused at the door. The beeping machines, the soft commands from nurses, the mechanical rhythm of life being sustained, it all hit Olive like a wave.

Justice lay still, chest rising unevenly beneath the sheet. A nurse was adjusting a monitor. Another checked the IV. They looked up briefly when the women entered, then quietly stepped out to give them space.

Justice opened his eyes, a slow, effortful motion. When he saw Olive, something flickered. A smile, not quite full, but enough to let her know he was still there. He lifted a weak hand and beckoned her closer.

She walked to him, her jaw trembling, and stood by the edge

of the bed.

"Hey there, Old Girl," he said, voice raspy but keeping with a familiar mischief. "Took you long enough. You bring snacks?"

Olive chuckled through the mist gathering in her eyes, lifting the dish like an offering. "Crackling cornbread," she said softly. "Still warm, Cayenne made it just for you."

Cayenne hovered in the doorway, tugging the edge of her sleeves.

"Well then," Justice said, squinting toward her. "I'd eat some, but I think my gut has already clocked out. Tell her thank you."

Cayenne choked a sob and crossed the room to his side, gently rubbing his knuckles. "You're welcome, old man. Always the smartass."

He smiled at her and winked. "Humor's the last to go. Don't let anyone tell you different."

Then he turned his gaze back to Olive, more serious now. "Come closer."

She moved carefully, uncertain where to lean, hesitant to interfere with anything that might be keeping Justice tethered to life.

"Closer than that," Justice said through his crooked smile.

She slid into the bed beside him, wrapping an arm beneath his shoulders as he settled into her embrace.

Justice gave a half-smile and whispered, "You feel good, stubborn girl, always insisting on sleeping in your own bed. I had to threaten to die just to get you back in mine." He gazed at Olive, and something shifted. The mischief faded, and the weight of time settled behind his deep brown eyes, eyes that seemed to be gazing from someplace his heart hadn't fully reached yet. For a moment, it appeared as though he was somewhere between where he lay and where he was headed. "This is it, Wife," he muttered. "I'm trying to adjust the schedule, but I think I'm about to clock out for real."

"Don't talk like that," she whispered, her voice quivering. "You don't get to leave me like this."

"I don't want to," he replied. "But my body's already halfway up the road. Just waiting on my soul to catch up." He exhaled, long and slow. "I need to tell you a few things. First, there's a letter on the coffee table at the house, make sure Janelle gets it. She needs to know. Needs to understand things from me, not just from you."

Olive nodded, her face buried in his shoulder.

"And keep building. The barn. The porch. Our legacy. Keep the garden blooming, too. Don't stop because I'm gone. You hear me?"

"I hear you," she said. "But I'm not ready."

"I know. Me neither. But if we waited till, we were ready for every damn thing, we'd never have started." He coughed lightly, a rattle deep in his chest. "Now, listen up, girls. I've got my punch list."

Justice's hand drifted toward Cayenne. "Tell Julien, I am proud of him. Smart as hell, and a good boy." He paused, his eyes flicking toward the ceiling for a breath. "Tell him I'm sorry..." He didn't finish the sentence, but the weight of it hung in the air, a quiet confession, a temptation toward a truth long buried but now brushing the surface, just out of reach.

Cayenne nodded, tears streaming freely now. "What *you* have to be sorry for?"

"Hmm. I didn't get to say goodbye..." Justice let out a breath that almost sounded like a chuckle, squeezing Olive's hand, he whispered, "Olive. I'll still be around, just not in dusty coveralls. Whenever you need me, just sit on the porch and wait. I'll come. You might not see me, but you'll feel me."

He grew quiet for a moment, then added, "Tell Red not to mess up the church. Tell Mildred she did a great job with my brother. I also liked the red velvet cake; just try not to overbake it next time. Make sure Caesar gets his runs so he doesn't get too lazy, he's old, but he still thinks he's the sheriff of Oakwood. That dog'll start running the place without me if you're not careful. Tell Marcus to stop using my tools and pretending they're his. And, Olive, you're always the brains behind the business, so I'm not hauling worry over to the other side about legal issues. Between what your Pops passed down and our daughter's sharp instincts, you've got all the help you need."

Olive pushed out a gentle laugh, pressing her forehead to his. "I love you, Justice Goodman. Ever since I barreled into your chest on the hill, even when we were apart, I couldn't quit my love for you. You've been more than a husband; you are my refuge and my ride or die. Even though I always believed I could do things on my own, I always wanted to do them with you."

He inhaled, shallow now, and gasped, "Slide in tighter with me, girl. I want to go like I came into this world, cradled in love."

She held him, felt the slight weight of his arm draped across her belly. Felt the rise and fall of his chest slow, then still. The room went quiet.

Cayenne, who had remained by the bedside, now leaned down and kissed his temple. "We've got it from here, old man."

A nurse returned, quiet as a breeze, and placed a hand gently on Olive's shoulder. "We'll give you as much time as you need."

Olive didn't respond. She just held her man.

Outside the window, a single beam of sunlight broke through the window blinds and lit up the floor by the bed. The room smelled faintly of cornbread. Justice's soul had caught up with his body, and he went on up the road. What remained was his punch list, now Olive's to carry. Woven into it was their love: every breath, every memory, every crack of light on the porch to come.

# SIX

# RECKONING

June 18, 2003– 1:17 p.m.

OLIVE WAS LOST in thought, barely noticing the world around her, until the screen door creaked open behind her. She stayed perfectly still at the familiar sound. She recognized her brother-in-law's gait, Judge "Red" Goodman. Slow and deliberate, soaked with reverence but never enough regret. Red always wore the collar starched, but Olive had lived long enough to know starch covered wrinkles.

Measured footsteps creaked over the porch wood. "Olive," Red said gently.

She faced him but didn't answer.

"My God, Olive. I heard. I came as soon as I could."

Still nothing.

"I'm so," Reverend Red's Bible hung loose in his hand; more shield than comfort.

"Don't say," she cut in, rising so fast the repurposed truck bench scraped loudly across the porch planks. Her demeanor was stoic, her eyes fierce with mourning and something else. Something bracing. "Our daughter is coming home to a funeral," Her voice cracked. "She's coming home to bury her father. And maybe…" she hesitated. "Maybe more than that?"

Red's eyes shifted. "What do you mean?"

"She'd been asking questions lately. Justice wanted to tell her about her adoption, but he never got the chance." Olive's voice thinned, brittle around the edges. "He was circling it. I could feel it, especially these last few days. There was something he needed to say, something heavy. But instead of speaking it, he wrote it down. Left it sitting on the coffee table like a final offering. And now I'm the one left to make sense of it all. To stitch it together."

Red stepped closer but didn't speak.

Olive narrowed her eyes. "He said we had to tell her; she deserved to know the truth before she wed. But Red, there's something he never said. Something he wouldn't name. And now that he's gone, I'm wondering…" Her voice trailed. "Why did *you* bring her to us? Why us?"

Red looked down at the floorboards. "Legacy Family Services… they had strict rules, files had to stay sealed, closed–

it had to be that way. That's why I was adamant– no questions. But when Eva came to me…"

Olive's eyes widened. "Eva?"

Red nodded, shame rising in his chest like heat off asphalt. "She told me she was pregnant. Said the baby was mine." His voice caught. "I panicked. Told her she couldn't keep it. That I couldn't… I was already married, already in the pulpit. I sent her away… to take care of it."

He paused, swallowing something sharp. "But she didn't. What I didn't know then, what I found out later, was that she was pregnant once before and was forced to terminate the pregnancy. She swore to herself she'd never do that again. So, she left town. I thought for good. We agreed. She stayed with a cousin out near Yellow Springs, but kept popping up for 9 months, hiding her belly behind an oversized coat. I tried to change her mind, until it was too late. She had the baby. Then came back–for good; holding everything I tried to bury in her arms."

"And you chose us."

"More like I heard from the Lord. I knew my brother's injury meant he couldn't father children, and I knew you… I knew your heart was ready for one. So, I asked the agency director to make your application a priority, you and Justice," Red said. "The social worker quietly bent the rules."

He paused, the weight of what he was about to say pressing into the quiet. Then he looked at her, his eyes clouded with something more profound than regret. "I didn't tell Justice who the baby belonged to. I made him promise. No questions. It was the only way." Red's voice cracked then, barely perceptible, but Olive caught it. "He was a saint that way," he went on. "Carried his questions like a breastplate. Held them tight to his chest, never flinched. He wanted a baby more than he wanted to know the story behind her birth. Wanted to be a father more than he needed the truth. And I let him."

Olive sat slowly, as if her knees buckled under the weight of it. "Red…" she whispered. "She has so *many* questions," Olive repeated slowly. "Not the kind we could brush off with a bedtime story or a Bible verse. Real-life questions. Grown-woman questions."

Red didn't speak.

"She's been going through old photos," Olive went on, her gaze narrowing, voice steady despite the ache behind it. "She held on to one from her first Christmas. No writing on the back. No hospital bracelet. No story to go with it. Just a baby, already bundled, already here." She paused.

"She didn't ask outright, not then, but I saw the yearn in her eyes. She looked at me like she was waiting for the story to unfold on its own." Olive's voice wavered. "And I didn't have one. She knows that I keep everything, Red. I've saved locks of her hair, baby teeth, report cards, and Mother's Day cards with stick figures drawn in crayon. But not that. Not the beginning. She asked me about her birth, her weight, how long was labor, what time she was born, who the doctor was, and family health history, things she needed to know for when she has children of her own... All the details mothers are supposed to remember. And I, I couldn't give her any of that, at least, honestly." She let out a breath that was almost a sob. "I gave her love. But not the truth. And truth is—I don't know why we were waiting to tell her."

Red looked down at his feet.

"Justice said we needed to tell her before she married that she deserved to know. Said she'd been chosen, not by chance but for a purpose. But he never told me all of it. It was always like there was some understanding between you and him. Just said... There were things even he didn't know." Olive's eyes locked on his now. "But you. You've always kept something back. I felt it, but didn't press."

Red sighed, long and low, like something ancient and brittle inside him had finally cracked. "Sis, I didn't join the military out of patriotism," Red began slowly. "I enlisted for a paycheck. You don't know what it's like to hide in those granite North Korean mountains, cold and trembling, huddled with the 503rd at Kunu-ri. We mixed gasoline with liquor to keep the trucks running, and sometimes we drank it ourselves to stay warm during the cold weather. Then, the Chinese came. Surrounded us. Our planes mistook their foxholes for ours. We were under fire from both sides. At night, it was screaming. Guns, bayonets, men crying out for mothers. I saw and did things I never told a soul. My brother understood that kind of muteness. He never pressed me for more than I was willing to give."

Olive's eyes didn't move. She was listening but guarded.

"I promised God if He let me live, I'd serve Him the rest of my life." He exhaled hard. "So, I came home, found a church, and joined Solidarity Methodist. That's where I met Milly. She was strong, devout. Came from a long line of preachers. She groomed me for the pulpit. It gave me structure and helped me rise in the community. But before all that…"

Red swallowed hard. "Before that, there was Cayenne. You remember. We weren't steady, but it was real. And when it ended, I thought it was over. I didn't know she was carrying my son."

Olive exhaled sharply, her brows furrowed. She shook her head, not in disbelief, but in quiet acceptance. This part of the story wasn't new, but the truth was still landing, rearranging things she thought she had already sorted out. It was like noticing a flaw in a painting she had looked at for years.

"I clung to the church, and to Milly, to what I believed was my calling. And then came Eva."

"Eva…" Olive echoed.

"She came to the church. Broken, angry, drinking. I tried to help through scripture and prayer. We met. Again, and again. And one day… we stopped praying. We started sinning. I fell, Olive. And from that fall came a baby girl. The baby I handed over to you and my brother, the baby you named Janelle."

Olive felt the shift. "You gave her to us," Olive said again. "And we raised her like she was ours. She *is* ours—never felt otherwise. And now…"

The adoption was sealed, locked away tightly. If I'd told Cayenne, she would've told you, and that would have brought the truth into the light. I didn't know how to hide it without destroying everything.

"And you waited this long?" Olive asked, her voice rising.

"I thought it was buried," Red said, near tears. "But some things don't stay buried. Do they? Instead, they rise. She's about to marry the son I fathered from a love that didn't hold."

Olive stood, trembling, her voice breaking. "You let us raise her with half a truth. You let her love your son with a whole heart."

Red didn't answer. He only nodded, heavy with guilt.

"I have to tell her now," Olive said at last. "Because I've been the one holding her all this time. I may not have been the first to cradle her, but I was the one who kept holding on, through every fever, every fall, every heartbreak. And I'll be the one who holds her when this truth breaks her into pieces."

Somewhere between sorrow and something older, something sweeter, a scent rose in her mind like perfume on a summer breeze, that day's joy. The day she became Janelle's mother. It hadn't come from a hospital bed or a birthing wail; it had come from a waiting room, Legacy Family Services, a signature, a whispered prayer she didn't say out loud.

Even now, decades later, beneath the weight of unraveling

truths, that moment tugged at her soul like a hymn she never forgot. Olive leaned into her grief, going with its current, searching for the bend where joy once flowed. And this joy, the daughter given to her and Justice, had come like a river blessing after drought, wrapped in grace, unexpected and deeply needed.

# SEVEN

# SECRETS WRAPPED IN A ROSE-COLORED BLANKET

OLIVE WORE AN oversized straw hat and green overalls, dirt under her nails; she stood out like a party host among the beautiful sunflowers in her garden when the telephone rang. The sharp, shrill sound from inside the house made her drop her trowel. She hurried inside, heart pounding. "Goodman residence," she answered, breathless.

"Hello, am I speaking to Mrs. Olive Goodman?" The voice stopped her breath cold. It was familiar, not the tone, but something behind it.

"Yes, this is Olive Goodman."

The woman on the other end softened. "Mrs. Goodman, this is Coreen Lyford from Legacy Family Services. We matched your application with a new birth; we have a baby for you. She was born yesterday. We hope you might consider fostering her. Her time in your care will count toward the adoption process, should you choose to move forward."

Olive clutched her chest. "Yes. Yes, we'd love to foster her. When can we come to meet her?"

"I can set an appointment as early as tomorrow. I must inform you that this is a unique situation. The birth parents' pastor, who has temporary custody of the baby, has requested to interview the prospective parents, providing our social worker with specific information about expectations regarding adoptive parents before terminating parental rights. In this case, the agency has considered their desires part of the qualification process. As agency director, I am making every effort to meet the birth parents' requirements, most of which relate to ethnicity, religion, and proximity to Dayton. The conditions I've stipulated are at their request."

Olive hesitated only for a moment. "We'll come. And the mother? Will she be there?"

A pause. "No, ma'am. This is a closed adoption; the Probate

Courts require that the records be sealed after the adoption is finalized. The birth parents wish to remain anonymous, Mrs. Goodman." The call ended with Ms. Lyford providing details and times.

Still clutching the receiver, Olive whispered a thank you to God, then skipped outside, calling for Justice.

On the day of the meeting, the sun had risen like it knew something sacred was on the horizon. Birds sang praises to their Maker, trees danced in the cool, forgiving air, and even the traffic seemed to move at a processional pace, every light turning green like a quiet blessing.

Olive wore a belted yellow shift dress and brown kitten heels. She appeared calm on the outside but was storm-tossed within. Justice walked like a soldier beside her in a brown leather blazer, a striped nylon shirt, gabardine pants, and freshly shined shoes.

They barely spoke on the way to the adoption agency. Still, it felt like everything around them was saying, "This moment matters."

The traffic moved in harmony with the breeze. The couple pulled into the parking garage of Legacy Family Services, exited the Buick, and walked hurriedly until they reached the grand oak door at the building's entrance. Pausing there, Justice reached for Olive's hand and held it. "You ready for this?" he asked.

Olive nodded, eyes forward, voice steady. "I am. Are you?"

she whispered.

Justice didn't answer right away. Olive knew the look. She had seen it the night before, when the poison had come calling. He'd stood at the sink, staring at the cabinet where the bottle used to live. It seemed as though the past was pressing in on him. But he didn't reach for it. He pressed his palm into a fist, the same one she touched now, and held on. No drinks. No detour. Just this, a second chance.

Once inside, the receptionist offered a hushed greeting and called for Director Lyford over the intercom. She met the anxious couple in the lobby with a gentle smile and a brown pocketed folder filled with papers tucked under her arm. She guided them down a hallway lined with watercolor paintings of families and cherubic babies.

Just before opening the door to a soft-lit room, she paused and turned to them. "I want to thank you both for coming. Before we begin, I want to be as transparent as possible, as this case has several delicate aspects. Nothing alarming, just threads that ask for care."

Olive glanced at Justice. He shifted his weight.

Lyford's voice lowered. "I will guide you through everything. We believe deeply that this match is the right one. That this child was meant for someone who could carry the weight of love with both hands." Then she opened the door.

Under ambient lighting, Reverend "Red," Judge Goodman stood, holding the baby. The infant was wrapped in a rose-colored blanket, wailing, her tiny fists curled like punctuation marks. The reverend rocked gently, murmuring something neither of them could hear. He looked up as his brother and sister-in-law entered. His eyes met Olive's first, then dropped. Justice froze.

Red cleared his throat. "She does not have a name yet." He said, his voice cracking.

Instinctively, Olive walked towards the small bundle and held out her arms, quavering as she reached for the child.

"I think she's hungry," Red said. "She tears up when I hold her."

Justice took a slow breath. "What are we walking into, Red?"

Red didn't answer. He just stepped forward and released the baby into Olive's arms. The cries began to fade. "You'll raise her?" he asked.

Justice looked at Olive.

She nodded. "As our own. Look at her, she's beautiful." Olive leaned in. The baby's eyes blinked open—spirited, too knowing. Something flickered in Olive's chest, a tug of recognition, like glancing into a mirror sideways. But she shook it off. Love would have to be enough. It always had been.

Red nodded, too. Once. "No questions, that's all that is asked." Then he turned and left the room, his shadow trailing behind him.

Olive looked down at the baby girl, now sleeping against her shoulder. Justice put his hand gently on Olive's back. They had walked into the fire and chosen to carry the light.

# EIGHT

# PRESS PRINCESS

June 18, 2003–2:23 p.m.

Chicago, Illinois

Zenith Sports Management Agency

JANELLE GRACE GOODMAN–five foot nine, with skin the color of spun honey and eyes like moss after rain, had two things in her purse: a tube of clear lip gloss and her BlackBerry, which was always charged, vibrating, and ready with a pre-written apology template. This latest episode would need more than a template. Sponsors were already calling.

Outside her office, in the adjacent conference room, her media team was glued to a bank of TVs, Fox Sports, ESPN, and the local affiliate on mute. The athlete's outburst was on every network loop. Silas Vaughn, star wide receiver and rising brand darling, was screaming at his coach on the sidelines, his mouth wide and hands flailing in anger. One still frame made him look unhinged.

Janelle retreated to her office, and the door clicked shut behind her. She slid out of her Louboutin pumps and sank her toes into the tightly woven carpet beneath her desk. It was a custom wool blend, slate gray with flecks of navy, installed when she took over the corner office, back when she thought control could be created with the right square footage and fiber density. The texture was soft enough to feel expensive but dense enough to muffle the weight of the crisis.

She flexed her toes into it now, grounding herself, letting the pile thread pull her out of the chaos just long enough to think. The TVs outside the glass walls hummed with half-muted commentary. Silas's outburst. Her name was mentioned once in a scrolling chyron. She crouched to reach inside her tote to grab the BlackBerry and rose back into the storm. "Pull the second camera angle," she told her assistant, Stanley. "The one where Coach Wright grabs his shoulder. Upload that to Silas' media portal. No caption."

Stanley hesitated. "That's not the one airing right now."

"Exactly," Janelle replied. "We're not reacting. We're redirecting."

She turned to her digital coordinator. "Cut together a 30-second highlight reel, mic'd up footage of Silas supporting teammates. I want it on our agency site within the hour. Label it Leadership in Motion. Subtle. Clean." Her BlackBerry buzzed in her palm. She held it up and thumbed it to life without looking away from the screens, expecting a sponsor rep or network contact. But it wasn't that. She noticed the call at 2:23 p.m., just late enough to be unusual, just early enough to mean something.

*Mom.*

She hesitated. Her mother rarely called during the workday. She always respected the boundary, a habit leftover from when Janelle tried to prove she could thrive in the city, away from small-town eyes and porch gossip. She picked it up. "Hey, Ma. I've got this current crisis under control. Just about to…" Impulsively, she reached into her purse and pulled out a single cellophane-wrapped Italian miniature hard candy, her favorite. The cool, sweet taste reminded her to breathe, if only for a moment.

"Janelle."

The way her name landed, Janelle, flat, quiet, stripped of informality, made her stop cold. "What's up, Mom?"

Olive's breath wavered on the line. "It's your father."

Janelle slid down into her chair. "Something wrong?"

"Justice drove himself to the VA this morning. He was having trouble breathing. He didn't come back. His heart…"

"Mom." Worry was anchoring her voice. "What do you mean he didn't come back? Where is he?"

"He's gone, baby. His heart gave out."

Silence pressed in heavier than the crisis she'd just untangled. "Mom. No. He was... he was fine," Janelle said, voice shaken. "We talked the day before yesterday. He said he was looking forward to this weekend. Said he couldn't wait to talk about..." Her voice caught. "He was excited. He finished the work in the barn. Told me not to have Julien's electrician bother coming over. He strung the wire himself..."

"I know," Olive whispered on the other end. "He was beside himself," she said, choking through tears.

Outside the glass-walled conference room, Janelle's team buzzed around the latest press crisis. She didn't hear a thing. Her eyes drifted to the press release blinking on her screen. The BlackBerry was still in her hand. The problem she'd just solved now felt distant. Insignificant. "Oh God," she whispered. "Mom, I'm coming home. Be there as soon as I can get out of here."

Still in her chair, she turned toward the window. Her reflection floated across the Michigan Avenue skyline, her green eyes gone gray in the concrete glare, her golden flesh dulled by grief. The sun caught her engagement ring, throwing slivers of light across the room. She lowered her head, one hand shielding her face from tears, the other tugging at a lock of her curly black hair, a habit she hadn't broken since childhood.

"He sounded good," she whispered. "Happy." But even as she said it, the memory shifted. He'd called twice that day. Once, to talk about ribs and homemade ice cream. Just an hour later, the second call was to ask if she was bringing the brownies she used to make in college. He never called twice. At the time, it made her smile. Now, it made her stomach twist. "Maybe something was on his mind," she said quietly. "He was circling something, now that I think about it."

A soft knock. Stanley, her executive assistant in charge of advertising, pushed the door open, holding a sleek white cup and saucer. The wet aroma of nutty espresso preceded him, curling into the room like a guest. "Thought you could use one of these," he said, setting it gently on the edge of her desk.

She looked up, her hand covering her mouth. Sadness dimmed her face.

"What's going on, Janelle?"

"I just need a moment," she said.

Stanley didn't move.

"You look like you need more than that. We've got this! That Silas thing'll blow over faster than it started."

She gave him a weak nod. "My father passed away this morning."

Stunned, Stanley adjusted his tone. "Oh, J," he said gently. "What can I do? I can call Travel, get you a plane, a train, whatever you need."

"Air," she whispered. Her neck was straining as she uttered, "I need to breathe. Give me a minute, please. I need to make a call." She reached for her phone. Missed calls from her fiancé filled the screen. Just as she was about to dial, the phone buzzed in her hand.

*Julien.*

"Babe, I've been blowing up your phone," he said as soon as she answered. "I just heard about Unc. I was having lunch with my mom at the restaurant. She didn't say much, just started getting food together to take to your mom's.". His voice cracked. "What do you need me to do? I will come and get you. Whatever you need, tell me." Julien's voice was gentle, low. "My mom will be with your mom until you get here. She will be surrounded by love. We got her."

Janelle nodded even though he couldn't see it. "I'll drive. It's faster than trying to book air, and the train will only stretch the time longer than I can bear." There was a pause. The city buzzed faintly outside her windows.

"I can meet you," Julien offered. "I'll be at your folks' house. Or wherever you need me. Get here safe, babe."

She closed her eyes. "Thanks, babe. I'll meet you there." A breath. "I love you."

"I love you, too."

# NINE

# GHOSTS AND A PARADE

June 18, 2003 - 8:45 p.m.

THE GOODMAN HOUSE loomed as a dark silhouette against the bruised blue-red sky, and a rustic haze settled over Oakwood. Janelle could see the lamp lights flickering through the windows as she drove through the neighborhood. A gentle breeze drifted through her open car window, accompanied by a symphony of crickets that seemed to welcome it; the sound wrapped around her like a warm hug. Although she was home, the night held an unfamiliar essence that made everything feel both comforting and strangely transformed.

She had driven from Chicago, the miles piling up as her mind jumped from one thought to the next; every hard question stuck in a continuous loop in her brain. Her dad is gone. It didn't seem real. Is this a bad dream? How was her mom going to survive this? The wedding. The date was only days away… They would need to postpone, or cancel, should they cancel?

Janelle coasted into the driveway, turned off the engine of her black Lexus, and slowly opened the door. She could hear muted voices through the screened windows, familiar and peppered with reverence. At that moment, she swore she heard her father's voice on the porch, caught in the flow of one of his stories.

She pushed her flats forward, the gravel crunching beneath them with each step. Before she could reach the porch, Julien appeared to arabesque down the stairs and met her where she stood. She realized then that it was his voice, animated and full of warmth, mingled with his father, Red, and Mac, the retired detective, one of her dad's closest friends.

Julien greeted her and wrapped her in his arms, forming a cocoon around her taut frame. "We're in this together, babe," he said softly. "I'll be by your side all the way. Whatever you need, tell me, I got you, J."

She wept against his chest. "I can't go in *there* right now," she said finally. "I know Mom's expecting me, but I just… let's wait for the visitors to thin out. I need a moment with my mom, but I'd prefer it to be away from all those people around. I know they mean well…" She looked toward the smaller cottage next door. "I'll go to the cottage, clean up, and collect myself. Will you grab my bag?"

Julien nodded. "Got it."

Something in the way he communicated, quiet, steady, and without a second thought, made her breath release in her chest. Not just the words, but the weight behind them. *Don't worry. Lean on me. I'm here.* His voice relaxed her for the first time all day, not entirely, but enough to prevent her from breaking.

The thoughts had pressed against her ribs, stealing every easy breath. But hearing Julien, feeling the unspoken promise in his voice, gave her one small breath of air. One moment of not carrying it alone. She let herself believe it. She let herself breathe.

Her fingers found the doorknob, cool against her palm, grounding her just enough to move. Janelle turned the doorknob and stood still for a moment. The cottage was familiar, not dusty with time, but alive with it. Her father had rebuilt this cottage with his hands from the bones of the old guesthouse. Every nail, every beam was an apology, a promise, a prayer, holding the life she left behind. And now she was back inside. She had been in and out of this space for years. Holidays. Long weekends. The slow, quiet mornings when she'd help her mother pick vegetables and wildflowers from the garden.

The scent of smoked ham hocks in a pot of prepped lima beans wafted from the kitchen, drawing her to the unfinished meal still resting on the stove, lid askew, burner cold. A few rinsed tomatoes were drained in a colander, and without thinking, she reached for one.

She padded over to the round oak table her father had built, its surface worn smooth by years of meals, homework, and whispered conversations. It had always been her favorite piece, not because it was perfect, but because it wasn't. One leg was just a touch shorter, rocking when she leaned into it. Justice had been too precise a craftsman to let a flaw like that stand; if he'd noticed, he would have fixed it. Her mother used to say that was proof he must've been drinking the day he made it. But to Janelle, that uneven leg felt like a secret handshake between them, proof that even the steadiest hands could falter, and that sometimes the things you love most aren't flawless at all. The table was him in wood and nails, solid, enduring, and still carrying a wobble no one ever bothered to fix. She turned her head to the window and noticed the closed record player, with a few albums leaning against it. B.B. King, Sam Cooke, and Ray Charles, the same ones her father always played when working on little repairs.

The wicker basket on the table hadn't always been there. Still, it was prominently placed, as if it were there temporarily. Janelle walked over and knelt beside it. Inside were photographs loosely bound with twine. Her breathing accelerated. She handled one with her in a frilly Easter dress. The Elder-Beerman tag was still safety-pinned to the sleeve. She remembered her dad making her spin in the living room, beaming with pride. *Twirl, then pose. Twirl, then pose.* When he hugged her afterward, she caught the smell of alcohol on his breath, but it didn't faze her. Not then. He was still her hero, the man who chose her dress, making her feel like the most loved girl in the room.

Another. A field trip snapshot. Third grade. He'd taken the day off to be the only dad chaperone, still in his work boots. She shifted to a seat on the bench by the table and let the tears come, steady this time.

***

The warm water trickled down her spine. Wrapped in a plush cotton towel, wet strands still clinging to her neck, she exited the bathroom, pausing when she heard a knock at the door. "Julien?" Still swaddled in the towel, she tiptoed barefoot to the front door and cracked it.

Eva DuBois stood there. Hair unkempt. Lipstick smudged, a wrinkled paper bag crumpled in one hand. "Hi, press princess," she said, squinting at Janelle with amused detachment. "Tragically, I ran out of Camels. It is a damn shame to be out of cigarettes and not able to smoke. Can you believe that? Nine months. Like it was court-ordered or holy, take your pick. Got a cigarette?"

Janelle blinked, her eyes puffy and sore from crying, her grip on the towel tightening. Her brow furrowed. "Nine months? Why, Miss Eva?" For a breath, the air between them seemed to shift, the way it does before a summer storm, just the weight you feel before you hear it.

Eva only laughed, a thin broken sound, and waved her hand as if chasing a gnat. "You look like a soap commercial. All dewy and dramatic." Eva looked past her into the cottage. "You back, huh? I could feel it in my bones. And I wasn't even tryin'." She held up the bag like it meant something, and the neck of a cheap bottle peeked from the crumpled edge. "Don't worry. Not food. I know Cayenne's got that covered. It's a little something to keep the ghost's company."

Janelle stepped back, unsure whether to laugh, cry, or slam the door. "Miss Eva, I don't smoke. Can I get you something else? Some water, perhaps? Or would you like to come in and sit for a minute?"

"Not yet," she said, cocking her head. Then she turned and stepped into the darkness without explanation, hips swaying, bag crinkling. "See you in the porchlight, baby girl," she called. And just like that, she was gone.

Janelle stood in the doorway, towel loosening, reality rearranging around her. A gravelly voice cut through the inky darkness, accompanied by measured footsteps crunching on the rocks.

"Eva?" A screen door slammed shut somewhere in the distance. Red's figure emerged from the shadows between the houses, his collar unbuttoned, and his jacket slung over his shoulder. He stared at Eva as if she'd stepped out of the past and landed wrong.

Eva froze mid-step, then turned slowly and theatrically. "Look who the Lord dragged in," she said. "Shouldn't you be somewhere blessing a pot roast?"

"What are you doing here?" Red asked in a disarming tone.

"Visiting the living. Unlike you." Eva hissed.

Red took a step closer, voice cold yet calm. "Don't stir up what's barely settled. Not tonight."

Eva's laugh was sharp and hollow. "Baby, you ain't settled a damn thing in decades. I just asked the press princess for a cigarette, not an altar call."

He looked at the bag in her hand and saw the bottleneck glinting. "Still carrying ghosts in paper sacks?"

"Better than hiding them in a pulpit." She snapped.

They stared at each other through the stiffening silence and years of neglect. Then Eva turned again, raising her bag in a mock salute. "You keep praying, Reverend. I'll keep dancing."

Janelle stood in the doorway, tightening the damp towel around her as she watched the scene unfold like a movie. The tension in the air had smuggled in unscripted lines and tension too raw for real life. Each word, each pause, each sharp glance seemed too exaggerated, too laden with subtext, yet too real to dismiss. She felt like she was eavesdropping on a private confession.

She had never heard her Uncle Red talk like that, not from the pulpit, not around a Sunday table, not ever. A Pastor was supposed to lift the broken, not throw stones at them. Wasn't he? The sour taste of confusion rose in her throat, murky and unexpected. She pressed herself back against the doorframe, the wood cool against her spine, grounding her as Eva sauntered away, humming something to herself.

***

The cottage settled into a hush after Eva's departure, the kind that feels heavier than noise. Janelle let herself sag against the doorframe, the towel slipping slightly at her shoulder, the day's weight unfolding around her. She was still catching her breath when a knock sounded again, softer this time, steadier. A knock meant for her.

She opened the door to find Julien standing there, steady and quiet, like he had always been. He didn't say much; he just held out her weekender bag from earlier. She took it, then looked up into those eyes that had never flinched, even when she fell apart.

They were college kids back then. She'd decided to leave Dayton, take Northwestern's offer, and everything that came with it. He stayed and chose the University of Dayton, opting for a future close to home. The separation almost caused their breakup. But distance has a way of doing what words won't.

Even then, it was his steadiness that drew her. His presence. He wore the kind of silence that meant something, never empty. The way he stood was like the ground that wouldn't give way. His skin was the hue of fresh-turned earth, and his hands were smooth despite his work in the trades today and back from undergrad. She stepped toward him and let her forehead rest against his chest. "I'll be ready in a few," she whispered.

When she returned, dressed and still composing herself, Julien reached out, and his hand found the nape of her neck; she could feel his steady pulse. The gentle rhythms calmed her. She closed her eyes. Julien covered her hand with his and led her toward the main house. They walked together, silent but sure, across the path to where mourners had gathered.

As they neared the edge of the driveway, another figure emerged from the front door of Justice's house, Red's wife, Mildred. Her stride was quick, and her posture was upright and disapproving. She had witnessed the tail end of Red and Eva's encounter from the porch. She reached Red first, leaned in, and whispered sharply, "This is a respectable gathering; we should keep it that way."

Then she turned to Janelle and Julien, her smile practiced, her eyes flicking briefly over Janelle's damp curls and the loose cotton dress clinging to her moistened skin, before softening just enough. "Janelle, dear," she said, "so glad you made it safely. Folks are starting to head out. Will you come inside now? Your mother is expecting you, and we are about to close with prayer."

Janelle looked at Julien, then gazed through the windows of her father's house that had an off-golden glow from the lamplights inside.

"It's prayer, babe," he said. "I got you."

She nodded once. "Yep."

Red, Mildred, Janelle, and Julien entered the house together. The living room was filled with church members, friends, and neighbors gathered in a loose circle around Olive. Their hands were linked, and voices murmured low. When they saw Janelle enter, the atmosphere in the room shifted. Heads turned, and eyes softened. Some nearly bowed their heads in reverence as she passed.

Janelle's eyes found her mother. Olive rose slowly, and before the two of them could think, they rushed into each other's arms. They clung tightly, their bodies shaking. Olive stroked her daughter's relaxed curls to smooth them. Around them, a gentle chorus rose.

"That's alright, baby."

"God, comfort them and give them strength."

"O God, touch right now."

"Wrap your arms around them. Bring your peace, O God."

Red stepped forward and lifted his voice. "Let's pray." He bowed his head. "Holy God, we are here today to thank you. Thank you for Justice, your handiwork, a decent human being, a son, husband, father, brother, and a pillar of this community. Thank you for the time you graciously gave us with him on earth, the love he poured into his family, and the friendships he cultivated in this neighborhood. We look forward to that great reunion in the sky. Your word says, 'To be absent from the body is to be present with the Lord.' So, while we will miss him greatly, we know you make no mistakes. We look to you for healing and restoration. I ask that you bless this family, God. Strengthen and settle them. Thank you to everyone here today for offering your love, time, and hearts. Grant us your grace and mercy in the days to come in Jesus' name. Amen."

Janelle stayed wrapped in her mother's arms, her face

pressed against the familiar curve of her shoulder, the way she had as a little girl after bad dreams. She heard Red's voice rising above them, smooth, certain, stitching a prayer out of all the right words. But somewhere in the raw place between her ribs, a new unease rose. Is this the same man who just confronted Eva? She didn't lift her head. Didn't let go. She just held tighter, as if the only truth she could trust right now was the beating of her mother's heart.

Daughter felt mother shift and pull her closer. Olive's hand trembled once before she buried it in Janelle's damp curls, anchoring them both. A soft murmur of amens followed. People began to gather their belongings, hats sliding off hooks, and pans and dishes being lifted from the kitchen counter. As they left, many paused to rub Janelle's shoulder or gently pat Olive's back. Janelle felt every touch like a stone skipping across water, quick, gentle, and gone, none of it reaching the deeper places inside her, where the ache had already gone still and cold.

Cayenne and her helpers had quietly begun tidying up, plates stacked, crumbs brushed into napkins, trash bags opened with practiced hands from Cayenne's Creole Table. As the movement rippled toward the door, Mildred stepped forward again and gently cleared her throat. She announced, "There will be a memorial service in a few days at Solidarity Methodist. Final arrangements are forthcoming."

Heads nodded, followed by a few murmurs of appreciation. Someone whispered, "Good church."

Voices faded as the house began to empty. The door opened

and closed again and again. And then, quite returned. Olive and Janelle remained embraced, seated on the sofa, their foreheads nearly touching.

Cayenne was drying her hands with a kitchen towel when she paused near the front window. "Good Lord!" She shouted.

"O Lord, really, today? What the hell is it now?" She hurried to the porch, and the others followed, drawn by the commotion outside. Flashing lights glowed against the dusk, red and blue pulsing not with urgency but honor. A police escort rolled slowly down the street, followed by a procession of cars. Community members, both young and old, leaned out windows, waving hand-painted signs and honking their horns.

"Justice, we love you!"

"We'll miss you, Justice!"

Some clapped, others called out his name with reverence and laughter.

Janelle stepped onto the porch with Julien, Olive, and Caesar behind her. Her hand touched her mother's again as Julien's hands touched her shoulders. Olive smiled through her grief, faint but noticeable. Her husband's legacy didn't need a eulogy; it had a parade. They stood in the porchlight, watching the love roll by. And the porch held space for every tear, every touch, and every hallelujah.

# TEN

# SNEAKY SPEED BUMPS

June 19, 2003

THE MORNING AFTER the parade moved differently, softer but still charged. Olive sipped fresh coffee from her favorite cup while Janelle, wrapped in a blanket, leaned back beside her on the repurposed truck bench. She relaxed, contemplatively, lost in the old stories her mother unspooled like thread.

"Wow, Mom," she said, laughing. "You bit Dad on the lip that day on the hill in The Bottom?"

Olive chuckled; a sound wrapped in memory. "It was a

default reaction. I had to slow him down somehow. I liked him, Lord knows I did, but I was scared that if he sandbagged me, I'd sink before I knew I was under. Your daddy was a big tease. Biting him just made him like me more. It was like I earned my chops, right there with my teeth," she said, laughing deep in her belly.

Janelle smiled through a veil of tears, affirming how much she loved the way the two of them loved. "Hmmm, different but alike. Mom, you've taught me so much from the way you love."

Olive grew quieter then, her voice finding a different register. "The war left wounds in your father that the medals couldn't cover. Some of them weren't visible, but they never stopped aching. His drinking was a scar he couldn't bandage, and it festered for a time. I almost quit my mind, quit my heart, on marriage altogether. I was determined to find my own way. Baby, I wasn't very tolerant when he took the teasing too far, and the drinking made it worse. That part about us, me, taking you, and leaving your dad. That was after he hoisted me up on the hot stove, playing rough, acting a plum fool. I bit him clean on the top of his head, came away with a mouthful of that coarse black hair and scalp. He was horsin' around. Me? I was out for blood."

"Oh, Mom really?"

"Really, I did. Another time, he came home drunk after hog huntin' and passed out on the couch. Rolled clean off the sofa and cracked a glass on the coffee table. I picked up the pieces while his throat vibrated in his sleep and arranged 'em around his neck. Part of me hoped he'd roll over and slice his neck on the cut glass, save me the trouble of doing something I would regret later. I'd had my fill of the drinking. It wasn't just wearing him down, it was winding 'round him slow, like a vine that don't quit 'til it's choked the life out of whatever it clingin' to. I could see it in his eyes, the way his laugh lost its shine, the drag in his step when he thought no one was looking. That's when I took you and left Justice behind for a while, hoping distance might save us both. Stayed at Ms. Bea's house after Horace Jr. took it over; his wife was kind enough to take us in. It wasn't easy. And thank God your dad didn't roll. You didn't have to grow up without your father or mother; I'd be in jail, carrying the weight."

She looked down, smoothing the hem of her skirt with slow, deliberate hands. "You know, baby girl, sometimes leaving is an act of love, too. Separation gives people time to find out who they are and what matters most, what they are willing to put up with, and what they must let go. I needed him to know that my heart wasn't something to be taken lightly. That your safety, my sanity, they were worth fighting for."

Janelle listened intently.

Olive smiled softly, a little sadness showing up in the lines around her eyes. "I came back because he changed. Your father is not one for speeches or grand gestures, but he changed. He built the cottage with his own hands, every nail a promise. He wanted to care for me, not just claim me. And I needed to be cared for, seen and heard, not just tended to like some pretty thing you polish and set on a shelf, watching the legacy take shape from a single point of view."

"There's a world of difference between loving a woman and keeping her. I wanted my hands in the work, my say in the plans, my fingerprints on every brick of what we built. I reminded him of that, over and over, hoping one day he'd know the difference too. And he got it, eventually. That's how we survived–plain and simple." Olive paused, her voice subordinating under her breath as if holding on to every word. "Justice, he fought for a second chance. And in the end, I gave in, not because I had to, but because he earned it."

As she gazed out at the road, her voice softened. "Baby, about your dad and me. Sometimes, leaving is the truest kind of love," she said. "Not because it's easy. Because it's the only thing that tells the truth. In the end, love led me back to him." She went quiet for a beat, the weight of it hanging between them. Then, with a slight shake of her head, she squinted at the street ahead. "I don't like those speed bumps," she said, almost to herself, her tone shifting lighter. "Never did. They sneak up on you."

"What? Mom, come back, where are you?"

"I'm here," Olive said. She sipped again. "Just thinking about the parade. I loathe the speed bumps they put in on this road, but last night, they slowed folks down enough to float. It was really nice."

Fog rolled over the Miami River, curling above Liberty Lane

like vapor in cold air. Cayenne's van rolled into the drive, its headlights scattering through the mist. The vehicle came to an abrupt stop. Cayenne pushed open her door and hoisted herself out, holding a steaming pot. The aroma of shrimp and grits wafted in the air. "Speed bumps," she said, cursing in the same breath, hopping up the porch steps. "I hate those things."

"I know you do," Olive replied. "Hot as a firecracker, you were always blazing through here, late for work, dropping off Julien. You haven't slowed down since."

The brume lifted slowly, revealing the old swing, the repurposed truck seat, and the black lacquer card table. Olive's gaze wandered across the borders of purple diamond shrubs and the great Angel Oak. She smiled.

"Let's eat," Cayenne sang. "Cheesy biscuits, and shrimp and grits. I ain't heading to the East Side till later, my people got it covered."

Janelle heard the screen door creak and turned. Julien emerged clean-shaven, smelling like tobacco and vanilla. She raised her brows and pointed at him. "Dang, dude. You got breakfast radar?"

"Hi, babe," Cayenne gushed at her son. "Figured you camped out here."

"Is that why you cooked?" Janelle teased.

"I cooked for ere' body, little Miss Fancy Press." Cayenne motioned, "Come on. Let's eat on the other side of the porch, away from your nosy neighbors."

Caesar let out a groan.

"Is he dead?" Cayenne asked, alarmed.

"Who?" Julien said.

"Woof woof. That dog. His legs are straight up like he's embalmed."

Julien laughed. "That's his sleeping position. He's fine. Uncle Justice used to run him at dawn. I'll take him near the barn and let him stretch."

While he disappeared around the porch, Cayenne launched into a memory. She shifted her eyes toward Janelle. "You remember that time I caught y'all tryin' to kiss? I mean deep in it, mouths open and everything. You couldn't have been more than seven."

Janelle gasped. "No, you *didn't!*"

"Oh yes, I did. I told y'all, 'Cousins don't kiss!' You two looked like I dropped a bomb in your sandbox. Everyone told me to leave y'all be– it was innocent. Didn't look like it to me. Looked to me like y'all had been practicing." Everyone laughed. Olive held her breath.

Just then, Janelle noticed a shadow at the edge of the driveway. A ghostlike figure leaned against the post.

*Eva.*

"Miss Eva!" Janelle called out, leaning and waving over the banister. "You want some breakfast?"

Janelle glanced at her mother as if to ask permission. She noticed how Olive tensed on the porch as Eva moved slowly forward, her face bare, no hat, no makeup, just her graying curls and that worn, striking skin. Her reaction seemed raw, as if she were allergic to the closeness.

Eva offered a faint smile. "Hey, press princess. No, thank you. I'll leave the ghosts sleeping today. It's a good day."

Then she turned, slow and sure, as if walking back into a fog only she could see.

Olive didn't move. She watched until Eva disappeared, then exhaled through her teeth. Olive pulled her shawl tighter across her chest, steadying herself in the hush Eva left behind.

***

The crunch of gravel echoed as they finished up breakfast. Tall and lanky, the visitor wore worn boots and a crisp white tee under a navy work shirt. He walked with a deliberate rhythm, as if someone raised with good manners had also been given bad timing.

Olive spotted him first. "Well, look what the cat drug in."

Janelle squinted. "Who's that?"

"Marcus Cook," Olive said. "One of your daddy's workers." Used to trap coons with him, too, and beat every man on the porch in bid whist, more than once."

Janelle stood, brushing biscuit crumbs from her lap.

Marcus reached the porch steps and removed his cap. "Morning, Ms. Olive. Janelle, Ms. ...."

"Boudreaux," Cayenne said smoothly. "Julien's mother."

"Right. Ooh, you must be Red's wife?" Marcus asked.

"No, baby. Not Red's wife. Just Julien's mother," she answered, with a smile that could cut one of her cheesy biscuits.

He nodded politely, eyes steady and unreadable. There was something weathered in his gaze, young in body but older around the edges. "Didn't mean to intrude," he said. "Just heard the commotion last night. Thought I'd come by and see if y'all needed anything." He looked at Janelle. "Your daddy taught me how to sit still. Not many folks can do that."

Olive narrowed her eyes as the young man approached. She watched Janelle tilt her head, and search the visitor's face, for a time, perhaps a memory.

Before Olive could say anything, Julien appeared at the edge of the porch, frozen in the moment he saw Marcus, who had been a thorn in his flesh from their college days. Olive noticed the slight stiffening of Julien's shoulders, the way his jaw set like someone bracing for something old and unresolved. He didn't speak, but the tension in his stance said plenty.

Marcus tipped his cap. "Julien."

"Marcus." Julien's voice was even.

The glances between the two men clearly announced something unspoken. However, Olive did not fully understand its shape–something that lingered from years ago, something unfinished, perhaps. She cleared her throat, filling the silence before it turned heavy. "Your daddy got Marcus out of a bad turn," she said evenly. "Boy had a track scholarship to University of Dayton; ran like he had wings... until he didn't."

Marcus gave a faint smile. "Tore my Achilles. Lost the scholarship. Dropped out. I started doing dumb stuff and writing checks I couldn't cash. Ended up locked up."

Janelle blinked. "Wait... what?"

"Justice bailed him out," Olive said. "Put him on a crew with Goodman Homes. That was the start of the turnaround."

"Yeah," Marcus nodded. "He gave me a hammer and told me to show up or stay lost. I chose the hammer."

"Then he went back to school," Olive added. He finished his business degree. Rehabs houses now!" She said with a wide grin.

Marcus gave a humble shrug. "Just trying to pay it forward. Justice didn't ask for anything back. Said I owed it to myself."

Julien crossed his arms loosely, and Olive noticed the shift, the slight square of his shoulders, the way his feet planted with more firmness than before. He offered a polite nod, but his eyes stayed locked on Marcus like a man scanning a memory for signs it could be trusted.

Olive didn't miss the flicker of something between them. She wasn't sure if it was old pride or fresh suspicion. But she could feel it rising like humidity before a storm.

Then, Marcus stooped without a word and plucked a bloom from the pitcher flowers near the porch steps. He turned it once in his fingers, then held it out, not to Janelle, but to her mother. "Justice said these flowers only bloom for folks who know how to listen," he said.

Olive took the blossom in her palm, fingers curling gently around the soft stem. "My husband said *that* did he?" she murmured, more to herself than anyone else. A small smile played at her lips, but behind it, her thoughts churned. Justice had said a great many things. Some tender. Some half-truths. All of them hers to carry now.

From the corner of her eye, she saw Julien shift again. Subtle, but sharp. She could only guess what he was remembering. Something was clearly bothering him. Justice once told her that Marcus and Julien had history, but he didn't give her much detail. Something about, boys on the track team. Marcus had heat in the chest at the time. Julien had held a grudge, the way some grudges grow even after the race is done.

She knew that kind of weight. Knew what it meant to see someone changed and still not be sure if the change would hold. She wasn't sure Julien believed in Marcus's new version. Porch-sitting, soft-voiced, full of "yes, ma'ams" and second chances. Olive wasn't sure she did either. But she knew the sound of a soul trying to make its way back. And Marcus, for all his history, hadn't flinched beneath the heat.

She watched as Janelle stepped back, her fingers brushing

the edge of the keepsake shoebox before lifting it into her arms. Olive knew that motion. The gathering of something heavy when the heart needed to be steadied. She watched her daughter cross the gravel path to the cottage, quiet and resolute. The porch itself seemed to exhale with her steps.

A beat later, the screen door to the cottage creaked open. Olive didn't move to follow. Some moments weren't for mothers to intrude upon. She sat still, the pitcher flower in her hand, its slender throat tilted slightly toward her as if waiting for her to speak first.

Behind her, she could hear Julien's steps trailing Janelle. She closed her eyes, just for a moment, and let the breeze press against her face. She would sit a while longer. Let the porch hold what it could. Let her daughter hold what she must. What Janelle didn't know, not yet, was just how much the porch had already held.

Olive was built stone upon stone from her past. The Bottom in West Dayton, stretched along the Miami and Erie Canal, a place some say once carried the Underground Railroad, wasn't just where she came from. It was in her, pressed marrow deep. The rough road wasn't what she'd wanted for Janelle, but if it came to that, she'd walk it beside her. The porch had seen it all, first heartbreaks, last goodbyes, and everything in between. Now, it held Olive in the hush before memory, as the past rose up like fog over the fields, waiting to be seen.

# ELEVEN

# THE BOTTOM

The Bottom, (also known as) *Hog Bottom*, West Dayton

1942-1945–give or take, the years got lost in the folds of memory

OLIVE RIDLEY WOKE to the colors of orange and red maples dappled across her bedroom wall, and the soft rustle of leaves against the magenta sky whistling through the cracked window. The branches swayed gently, whispering secrets just for the morning's get-up-and-go folks. She lay in her bed a little longer, soaking in the psithurism, until the cackle of chickens squabbling over feed pulled her fully into the day.

She snoozed to the pitch of her grandfather humming low

outside, mixed with the trickle of grain as he tossed it from his wide palms. She groaned and threw back the covers. "Dammit," she muttered, knowing she would have to answer for her slothfulness.

The morning fire in the parlor had warmed her room, but the cracked window let a sly chill nip at her legs. She rushed down the narrow hallway, her nightshirt swirling behind her like a cape. At the washbasin, she splashed cold water on her face, brushed her teeth in hasty strokes, and tied her curls into a haphazard knot. Her reflection flashed in the mirror, amber skin glowing against the pale morning light, eyes the deep, knowing color of walnuts. She didn't linger, no time for vanity, not when the race to the barn had already begun and her grandfather was ahead by a coon's age.

"Pops" had taken on the shape of fatherhood after Olive's mother left. George Ridley, a retired gambler who traded dice for deeds and became, if not respectable, then at least respected. He taught his granddaughter the kind of lessons no school could offer, how to bet wisely, spot a lie before it left a man's mouth, and survive when the world kept trying to knock her off her feet.

Olive's mother, Georgina, had left town, chasing a man who wasn't Olive's father, and headed east to the city that never sleeps, with a suitcase packed with promises she never kept. Olive only knew the rumors, a Welsh soldier, fresh from the war, who'd courted her mother and knocked her up in the cellar of a dank tavern and disappeared long before Olive took her first steps.

She raced back to her bedroom, snatched her overalls from the chair, swooped them over her flannel shirt, and tugged on her mud-caked mucks. She skidded through the kitchen, the scent of frying bacon curling up to meet her. Frey, Pop's former housekeeper, swayed to Billie Holiday crooning low from the radio, a gardenia pinned in her jet-black hair. She sang along, hips keeping time as she flipped potato cakes and stirred onions in a skillet.

Frey became a constant presence between the time Olive's grandmother died and her mother's departure. At the start, she was a charming yet cunning housekeeper who possessed the ability to sniff out money among a herd of musty hogs. She eventually became Pop Ridley's lover and wife.

Olive tiptoed toward the hot plate, fingers inching toward the biscuits. Almost as if she had eyes in the back of her head, Frey spun, spatula in hand, and smacked Olive's knuckles. "Sit down, gal. Eat proper," Frey chided. Olive detected more duty than affection in her voice. "Don't you run outta here on an empty belly!"

Olive rolled her eyes. "Gotta, keep it movin'," she quipped, ducking the scolding as she grabbed a biscuit and stuffed it in her pocket. She was halfway to the barn before Frey could lay hands on her.

Outside, the wind pulsed through her shirt, whipping her hair back and forth. She trotted past Pops, who barely spared her a glance as he tossed grain into the muddy troughs, snorting hogs crowding at his heels. "Morning, Pops!" Olive called, breathless.

"Morning, Olive," he answered, voice flat. "Little late this morning, huh?"

"Not really, sir. I still have time before school, no class, field trip instead," she said, respectfully but rushed. "I don't want to go on any dumb field trip anyway," she mumbled. "I got more important things to do."

Pop Ridley, never one to miss a good hand, taught Olive how to win. He built shanties out of orange crates and scrap lumber, quick-turnover rentals for the wandering workers who flooded Dayton after the war, drawn by factory jobs and the rough promises of northern streets. The tenants came and went, but they stitched themselves into Olive's childhood like quilt squares, teaching her to bluff, hold, and know when to fold.

By the time she was ten, she could slap cards with the sharks. Her oval face was calm as stone, her hands quicker than a prayer. Many nights she stayed up long past the hour a child should've been in bed, sitting cross-legged in the thick smoke and grounded laughter of Pop's parlor.

Her birthday gifts were rarely dolls or dresses. She unwrapped shotguns, rifles, and farm tools, gifts chosen not for play but for survival. Her favorite, the one she loved beyond reason, was the CJ-2A Jeep Pops gave her, a rattling beast of a machine, strong, dependable, and versatile. At the threshold of thirteen, Olive drove it to school and across the muddy fields when she had a mind to.

Olive was more than a granddaughter; she became a student of her Pops, learning the maneuvers of his survival. He had quit school before eighth grade, survived the hard lessons of the streets, and manipulated men who had nothing but fists and desperation. He was whip-smart in math, could tally a winning hand before the last card was dealt. In every game worth betting on, Pops played with an undeniable charisma, and to everyone's delight, Pops claimed his victories with triumphant flair.

As she studied him, longing to be like him in every way that mattered, she developed a fierce desire to emulate his effortless confidence and joy. He moved through spaces like royalty. When he spoke, even the animals twitched their ears. "Did you eat breakfast, girl?" he asked, eyes narrowing.

"I got a biscuit in my pocket," Olive shot back.

"Mmm hmm," Pops grunted. "Frey let you out without food in your belly?" His voice held a note of fondness, but something else too. The kind of tone a man used for a woman who fed him, kept his bed warm, and held his ear when no one else could. "Best get back in the house..."

Olive rounded the barn; the air was clouded with the scent of fresh manure and damp hay. December and January, her two cows waited, stoic and unimpressed, their dark eyes expressing plainly, 'Bout time, girl.' She grabbed the ropes from the hooks, looped them around the cows' hefty necks, and tugged them gently toward the hill.

The trail up from The Bottom was a mess of mud and slick rocks. Olive slipped, stumbled, but December and January pulled her upright with their stubborn, steady weight. The mound, a former burial site, smelled of churned earth and green things just waking. She kept her head down as she climbed, boots sucking at the mud, until she reached the crest.

She saw his boots before she saw his face. Justice. He stood above her, grinning that cocky, half-grown grin she hated almost as much as she secretly loved. "Hey, Justice," Olive muttered, refusing to blink first. "Get outta my way, please."

Justice's family owned the land behind the empty field. Pops was uncharacteristically late when bidding for the property, losing out to the Goodman family, who bought it cheaply from the Native Americans when developers refused to build near a burial mound. Justice's father, Horace Sr., saw value where others saw superstition. He brought back the land from the dead, raised livestock, and resurrected a general store that dealt in farm supplies, handmade tools, and local produce, an outpost that later evolved into a discount store, helping to build the family's wealth. The discount mart survived, but the field, now empty, was once filled with stories, the weight of bones beneath, and the dreams of those who dared to build upon them.

Justice was supposed to be out chopping firewood. But it was if he sniffed out Olive before he could see her, and lately, he lingered wherever she happened to be, hauling wood, mending fences, or just standing there like the world owed him the space. "You're late again, Olive," he said, his voice stinging with teasing.

"So what?" she snapped. "Don't start with me!"

"Olive Ridley. I'm gonna marry you," he said casually, as if marking it on a calendar.

She shoved him aside with a flat palm and led December and January to graze, her boots squelching in the soft earth. "Who said I wanna be married?" she called over her shoulder, with a dare in her look.

Olive was both pretty and tough, and tough because she was pretty, two truths that wrestled for space in her head. Her mother's abandonment had taken root deeply in her, leaving her with stubbornness, fierce independence, and the kind of pride that bloomed hard and fast when love proved unreliable.

Justice just watched her, her wild curls poorly tamed, her leanness, and unbreakable mouth. "You gonna love me one day," he said. "You just a girl. I'm a man. I see things you ain't even looking for yet."

"Seventeen don't make you a man," she barked, spinning around, chin high, "And three years don't make you smarter than me." She opened her mouth to slice him again, but the words died somewhere between her pride and her heart.

Justice stood easy, arms crossed, a slow, certain grin spreading like a promise. "I know what kinda man you gon' need. I'm gon' be that man. I'm gon' build houses all over this city one day. I'm gon' make you a happy woman." He didn't shout it, didn't plead. He just said it as if it were already settled.

Olive felt her breath catch fire in her chest. "Well, you gon' need more land and more money than my Pops," she hissed. "My Pops owns half The Bottom, cows, pigs, horses. He's already made a pile from his rentals. When he dies, I'll be rich too. You gonna have to have…"

Justice lifted a finger, pressed it gently to his lips. "Shhh," he said, soft and smug.

"Uggh," Olive gasped, outraged.

"You gon be my wife, Olive," he said, "as sure as black and white."

She scrambled to regain her footing, but her boots had a mind of their own. She stumbled, barreling into his chest.

Justice caught her easily, waiting arms wrapping around her.

"Well, damn girl," he murmured against her hair, "I ain't even built you a house yet."

His arms were strong, smelling of cut wood and sweet hickory. Her hands, trapped against his chest, trembled. She didn't know what to do with the want blooming fast inside her. She tilted her head up, and when their lips met, she bit him, a sharp, playful nip. Justice blinked back a tear, swiped his thumb across the bleeding cut, and, grinning, wiped the blood on her shirt, right over her heart. "Aww, come on, girl," he teased. "Let me kiss…"

"Was that a tear?" she mocked, trying to hide her burning cheeks. She pursed her lips and snickered, but even she could feel it-something had shifted between them, sharp and sure and undeniable as the morning sun.

***

The road that wound through The Bottom was unpaved and rocky for those who landed in Dayton before her, seeking hope and freedom after the Civil War. Amid the working-class legacy and the lingering scent of hickory smoke and warm mud, Olive learned resilience. From the porch, it was plain to see, the steadiness in her step, the way her shoulders carried both history and hope. That porch had watched her grow into herself, had listened to the stories that rose up from the road, and kept them, the way old wood keeps the sun.

Pops had taught her that every journey worth taking began hard and uneven, requiring something from you before it gave anything back. Olive had been forged in the fire of The Bottom, its lessons stitched into the seams of her soul, the quiet grit, the fierce hope, the stubborn faith that refused to die.

She knew the shape of a hard road, the way it rose to meet you when you had nothing left to give. It was the road she walked when her grandfather's heart gave out, and Frey, the woman he left behind-the grieving wife, and conniving step-grandmother, but never felt like family, set the lawyers on Olive like hounds.

That same road she walked was the one her mother hadn't stayed long enough to reciprocate the love that Pops gave. She left when Olive was a baby, chasing something Olive was too young to discern. And yet, years later, when Georgina reappeared with hollow eyes and empty pockets to claim the inheritance from her father's estate, competing against her stepmother and her own child, she was no match for the ones who stayed.

It was Olive who answered the call to aid her mother. First with what little she had, and later, with what she built. She supported Georgina through illness and decline, paid for the nursing home when Pop's money was long gone. The road asked much of her, but Olive learned to give without expectation, and in that, she claimed something deeper than forgiveness. Purpose.

Some memories have two faces, joy on one side and sorrow on the other, and the trick of living is learning to hold them both. But even Pops couldn't count some things. He never did learn to reckon the cost of a woman's lies. His blind love left Olive fighting battles he should have seen coming.

And now, the table was empty, the coins long spent, the lessons learned. Olive fought for what was hers in The Bottom, but the law favored the loudest voices, and Olive, without representation, was left with scraps of her inheritance and none of her home. Thrown from the only life she knew, she wandered for a time, her fading footprints and heart heavy as cement, until hope dared to stir again.

Hope carried Olive to Oberlin College on a scholarship offered by the National Council of Negro Women, a lifeline stitched together by women who had fought for civil rights and social justice, and for a future that stretched beyond their own. Olive clung to the dream of becoming a teacher with hands toughened by labor and a heart too stubborn to quit. Between semesters, she worked at Wright-Patterson Air Force Base as a tug and truck driver, her fingers gripping the wheel while her mind gripped the lessons she could not yet teach.

She saved as much money as she could after paying her necessities, living on little more than determination and grit. She even loaned money she had saved up for her education to kin who smiled widely when they asked and forgot to repay. When her savings dwindled, Olive had to let go of her dream of becoming a teacher like a bird released into an unforgiving sky. It tore something inside her, but it did not unmake her.

Instead, she turned her heart toward what remained. And there, waiting at the hill's crest, was Justice, the boy with the sawed-off grin and the hands that steadied more than just runaway calves. The boy who had once grinned at her through a cloud of kicked-up dust and said, plain as a vow, "I'm gonna marry you, Olive."

Justice wasn't a rescue. He was a reckoning. The stubborn root of her heart could wrap itself around when the world offered no softer ground. She learned to love him the way she had learned everything else, in the rough and tumble of living, in the long, slow labor of trust. She loved him first in The Bottom, where promises grew in crooked rows and still somehow bloomed. When he proposed, she blinked and still said yes. "I don't like you like that, Justice," she recalled, and just like that, she made up her mind

Now, her heart had no place to go but deeper still, into the life they had built together, stubborn and beautiful, set against the backdrop of Montgomery County's days gone by, of clattering cash registers, the bright whine of airplane engines, the smell of molten metal in the lighting factories, and the slow stretch of Oakwood farmland pressing up against the Miami River's dammed basin.

The Bottom had been her comeuppance. It was where she learned to fight and to forgive, often in the same breath. Only the clink of the memory remained, steady as a keepsake in her pocket, and it would sustain her.

From the porch, the years of it could still be felt in the boards, the heat of those hard lessons, the soft weight of her forgiveness. The wood had held it all, and would keep holding, long after she stepped away.

# TWELVE

# CELESTIAL WELCOME

THE COTTAGE WINDOWS streamed columns of light upon the hickory floorboards. Janelle was lost in thought. When she collected herself, she blurted out, "Marcus!" her tone breaking the tranquil mood.

Julien took a cautious step back; an eyebrow raised in curiosity. "Marcus?"

"Yes. Marcus Cook," she replied, nodding slightly as memories flooded back. "He was dating Fern when they arrested him for check fraud, coming out of a Dayton View jewelry store. When Fern heard about it, she dropped him like a bad dream. It's such a shame, I liked him. He had that delightful Southern gentleman charm, complete with smooth manners and that easy, warm smile that could light up a room."

Julien remained quiet, his jaw tight, listening in silence, his expression a mix of contemplation and unspoken thoughts as if he were navigating through a maze of emotions stirred by her words. "Hmmm, maybe, with the ladies, but his aggressive behavior, the need to dominate, while we were at UD, showed me his true colors. Maybe people can change. I don't know. I just never saw it in him."

Janelle sensed the subtle withdrawal in his posture. The temperature in the room hadn't changed, but the air felt different. She touched the edge of the diploma and then looked up at him, offering a small smile. She reached for his hand, curling her pinky finger around his and tickling it softly. "Hey, babe… I think we both could use some fresh air. Let's take a break. Why don't we walk over to the barn and see what my dad was up to?"

***

There was a sweet hush over the neighborhood. Janelle leaned into the tranquility Liberty Lane offered her like a sacred embrace. Her father's spirit was everywhere, she felt as if the divine had created a tabernacle for the angels to sing in joyful welcome, one of their own had returned to the heavenly fold.

Janelle assigned Mildred to stay at the Goodman home to oversee the drop-offs, food, flowers, and sympathy cards, a role she knew her aunt could easily slip into. Mildred ensured likely visitors were made aware that Mrs. Goodman needed her rest.

She hadn't slept in her bed for two days. First Lady Mildred made sure that the grieving widow rested comfortably in the room she sometimes shared with Justice.

Janelle and Julien closed the cottage door behind them and walked past the quiet porch. As they neared the barn, the couple paused at the large hickory doors. The warm June air flowed gently, caressing the Angel Oak's vibrant leaves. She felt her spirit lift. It was as though the gentle touch of nature rejoiced in harmony with a celestial celebration.

"Shall we?" Julien asked, his voice calm and reverent.

Together, they pushed the doors open. Janelle gasped. Inside the rustic structure, delicate sheer voile cascaded gracefully from the rafters, refracting the light in a soft, shimmering glow reminiscent of ethereal clouds of lace. Beneath the grand main beam, a beautifully adorned wedding arch beckoned, bordered by vibrant flower boxes bursting with color and a long, inviting wooden aisle runner.

"Oh my God. Oh my God," Janelle whispered. Her knees buckled, and she sank into a nearby wooden chair. Tears came fast.

Julien's eyes welled up, too. "Unc," he said softly.

A ladder creaked in the distance. A man was affixing a chandelier to a beam. As Julien moved closer, he recognized him. "Marcus?"

"That would be me," the man answered without turning.

"What… what's going on?"

Marcus climbed down slowly. "What's it look like? I'm hanging lights."

"I thought Uncle Justice said he didn't need my crew. This… this is a big job."

"He said you were busy. Didn't want to pull you away from your contracts. He called me. I've got a small crew and mostly work solo. We wired the barn, laid the fountain pipe, and helped him build the aisle runner."

Janelle joined them, wrapping an arm around Julien's waist. "It's beautiful. Like a dream."

Marcus smiled. "Here, let me show you," he said, extending his hand.

He led them to the corner of the barn. "Dining goes here, best light. Round tables are coming in, and the dance floor is marked out over there. Caterers will prep along the back wall. Everything fits. Even the reception. Outside, they're finishing tidying up the wildflower garden. The chairs and cocktail tables will be set up in the garden."

Janelle let go of Julien and gave Marcus a spontaneous hug.

Julien shifted and reached for her wrist. "You've got a wedding planner, babe," a touch of sarcasm in his tone.

"I do," Janelle said in a whisper. "She's coordinating, not constructing. This, this is different."

Marcus chuckled. "It's all Justice. He had a vision."

Julien forced a smile. "You've outdone yourself, man."

"Justice did. I just followed orders. That man pulled me out of the ditch, literally and figuratively. This is from him- all for his beautiful daughter."

Julien's jaw tightened, and a muscle twitched near his temple. Janelle saw it. "What's wrong?" she asked, stepping nearly nose to nose.

He hesitated. Shook his head once, slowly, a line forming between his brows. "Dude is way too invested, that's all." He tried to make it sound casual, but something in his tone curled with unease, like a wire pulled tight and humming.

Janelle reached for Julien's hand and squeezed it. "He was helping Dad. Quit being weird." She kissed his cheek, then turned back to Marcus. "Now, Marcus, what's going on over here?" she asked, pointing to the artificial vines sprawled across the wooden planks.

"A wall of vines and more planters for the pitcher flowers and orchids. Your favorites, right?" he said casually.

"The orchids are my favorite," she smiled, "but I've always been fascinated by the pitcher plant. Mom loves having them all around. We have a whole patch near the front porch. They catch insects and small creatures. When I was little, I imagined they could trap my dreams and keep them safe." She paused, "Goodness, Dad. Why aren't you here for this?" Her voice cracked as tears rose again, a moment of deep reflection washing over her. Julien pulled her close.

Marcus stepped back, brushing sawdust from his pants. "Sounds like you two have some talking to do," he said gently, "and I've got some bailing to finish up in the rear. The baler broke down, and it put us a little behind schedule. But we will be ready for the big day." He gave Janelle a soft nod, tapped Julien once on the shoulder, and slipped out the side door into the sunlit morning. The barn, hushed again, retained its silent joy and grief and tucked in tension. The distant porch seemed to whisper, its presence lingering, as always, like an old friend recalling memories.

# THIRTEEN

# PORCH WITNESS

THAT EVENING, the porch would witness much more. People arrived in gentle clusters, neighbors with dishes, old friends, cousins, coworkers, and Justice Goodman's war buddies. They all came through, to mourn, to pay their respects and remember. Because that is what they did on the porch, which reliably absorbed every whisper of the world around it, there would be laughter, long stories, playful jabs, and pauses so full that they conveyed more than words.

The porch watched as Julien and Janelle emerged from the barn, shoulders square, expressions composed. Whatever truths had been exchanged between the rafters, they carried something quieter now, something anchored. Their eyes scanned the yard where the gathering swelled, a familiar rhythm, like when Justice, the unofficial mayor of Oakwood, once held court.

Janelle searched for her mother. She seldom made an appearance when Justice was holding court. But this time was different. They came for his widow, for his daughter. The porch noted how Mildred moved about, eager to be useful, while Cayenne sat like still water beside Olive. Different as dusk and dawn, those two, bound by loyalty. Cayenne was security, silent and steady. She watched, present, ready.

"Hey, Miss Olive," someone said. "We are praying for you."

She nodded, a slight movement. "Thank you."

"Mrs. Goodman, if you need anything, please call me. You and Justice have always been there for me."

From the edge of the drive, a joyful squeal broke through. The porch turned toward it, Fern, her curls loose in the wind, running full force toward Janelle. The embrace was tight, true.

"Fern, girl, you made it! I'm so happy you came. Thank you, thank you!"

Fern glowed with the sun on her freckles. "Come hell or high water, I would be here for you, girl. My city never sleeps, but this? This mattered. Remember when your dad picked us up from that Wapatui party? His face, girl! You lied and said you were going to the library."

"I lied?"

"We lied! But you were the one who called him, drunk and scared."

They laughed, loud and unguarded, just like they had in college.

"How are you, seriously?" Janelle asked.

"Working like mad. Vegas is a hot real estate market right now, and I am capitalizing on all the migrations. I got my broker's license after we graduated and never looked back. Grad school wasn't for me. I hope we can catch up later. Anyway, I planned everything around the wedding, I wasn't going to miss it. But this? I'm sorry about your father, J."

Julien waved from the porch. "J, Fern, over here. Come, sit down!"

Janelle lit up. "Guess who's here?"

"Who?"

"Marcus."

"Marcus, who?"

"Marcus Cook. Your ex."

Fern blinked. "What is he doing here?"

"Helping my dad with the barn renovation," Janelle said, her voice all sparkly. "Girl, come on, I'll tell you all about it."

"Okay, now I need a cocktail," Fern groaned. "Julien is

waving us over. Let's sit before Marcus sees me."

A woman from Solidarity approached. "Hi, Janelle, I'm the head usher. Let me know if you need anything before or during the service."

Mac's voice boomed from the other side of the porch. He had a story, he always did. "Olive, remember when that girl crashed into your fence? Thought she was dead. Justice found her and called me directly. Wouldn't call it in. Said rookies couldn't handle it. You hosed her down till the medics came. Naloxone saved her. She's in Los Angeles now, trying to be a movie star."

"How do you know that?" Cayenne asked.

"Read it in the LA Times. The girl played a junkie, a nun, and a cosmetologist. Tried out for Pandora in Baby Boy, didn't get the part."

Fern overheard. "Loved that movie. Tyrese? Whew! I'd trade my snacks just to see him bare-chested."

Laughter rippled across the porch.

Red arrived, his demeanor a little cool for the atmosphere. "Who's the little birdie, Mac? You stalking that girl?"

"Man, I got the 411." He clapped Red's shoulder. "How are you holding up, Reverend?"

Red nodded slowly. "Trying to send my brother to heaven and keep demons from circling the living."

The porch took that in. Janelle did too, watching her uncle, but before she could dwell on it, Stanley showed up, phone in one hand and briefcase in the other, already discussing contracts.

Janelle hugged him, and after a quick agency briefing, pointed him to the food, and he was off like a hungry bear.

The sun began its golden retreat. Conversations braided joy and sorrow, the way they always did. Eva sat at the edge, cigarette in hand, mumbling something about nine months without a smoke not being a holy sacrifice. Cayenne watched from a distance, scanning the porch. She noticed Red's agitation. Glancing at Olive, she started to rise.

"Let her be," Olive whispered, eyes narrowing just enough to catch the shift in Eva's jaw. She'd seen that look before, Eva's fuse was short, and Olive wasn't about to let the truth tumble out here, not when it would land like a brick in the wrong place. "Don't need nothing to break," she said, more to herself than anyone else.

Janelle had been watching, and she approached gently. "Hi, Miss Eva. You hungry?"

"No."

"I'd be happy to fix you a plate…"

"Girl, I drink. I don't eat."

"I was just…"

"If I want food, I can get it myself."

Janelle hesitated. "You said something about nine months. And that it wasn't holy. Did something happen with my uncle? He was short with you. I've never seen him like that."

Eva didn't answer. Her eyes followed Bette Day, Justice's neighbor who was in the Women's Army Core during the Korean War. She avoided Janelle's question; instead, she focused on Bette Day as she puttered around in her yard. "Bette was burned in a grease fire. Lost her sight. Justice helped her. Helped her stay afloat after her twin sister died, and her land in Florida was foreclosed on. He gave her the land to park that double wide. Brought her food to keep her from trying to cook. He did that for people. Did it for Olive, too. Her grandfather died, and her step-grandmother didn't want her. Justice gave her a way out. He showed up. Red hides. Justice never did."

Janelle sat with that. The porch held its breath.

Behind them, laughter erupted again.

"Janelle, baby, come say hello to Clarice, your uncle Horace's daughter!" Her mother called out from a distance.

Janelle stood, her legs stiff. She squeezed Eva's hand and focused on her mother's direction. There seemed to be more there, buried deep. But for now, she would settle for cake and conversation.

Eva watched her go, then looked across the porch. Her eyes met Olive's. No challenge. No sorrow. Just a quiet knowing.

And the porch, its boards worn smooth by generations, bore witness to it all.

# FOURTEEN

# WHAT FOLKS SAY

FOG HUNG LOW over Oakwood like the loose hem on a dress. The sun hadn't yet pushed through the mist, and everything felt like it was holding its breath. Janelle sat on the truck seat, her father's favorite perch, wearing a loose cardigan over her pajamas. She was sipping coffee from his Best Dad Ever mug. The coffee inside had cooled, but she didn't care. The well still smelled like black coffee and something faintly outdoors.

Olive sat beside her daughter, a colorful throw folded over her lap, one foot tapping against the wood floorboards. They said nothing for a long time. Between them sat a tattered shoebox, its edges bowed, filled with paper clippings, letters, photographs, receipts, and curled envelopes. Some were barely held together with yellowed tape.

In front of them, the red and white wheelbarrow had been overtaken by pitcher plants, their long necks lifted skyward, as if they were waiting for a story to unfold. A faded wind chime whispered under the Angel Oak, the same tree Justice refused to cut down when he built the house. To the left sat the D100, the sunshine-yellow truck that still looked as if it were smiling. Olive took a sip of her coffee. "I never liked that wheelbarrow," she said softly.

Janelle smiled. "I like it. Always seemed like it was about to burst into song." They reached for the box at the same time. Olive's hand paused on the lid, not lifting it. She glanced sideways. "We could talk about it, you know. About your upcoming marriage. The family lines. What folks say."

Janelle didn't meet her eyes. "I know what people say. And I'm not interested in digging up bones that everyone's already made peace with."

Olive's fingers curled around the edge of the box. "But not everyone has."

"I just want the stories today, Mama," Janelle said, quieter now. "Just the memories."

A long pause. Olive nodded. "Fine. Just the memories." She let her daughter open the lid.

"He kept everything," Janelle said, lifting a folded paper. It was a receipt from the lumber yard dated 1958. "This for the porch?"

"Mmhmm. Cedar and walnut were his favorite types of wood. Said together, they smelled sweeter. I never smelled it. Just smelled like wood to me."

They both chuckled softly. Then Olive grew quiet again.

"Some things he never threw away. Even when I asked him to. Especially when I asked him to."

Janelle turned another envelope over in her hands, her thumb running over the corner where it had been opened and resealed. Each item was a story, a memory, a breadcrumb. This was the quiet place where love lived now, in fog, stories, in a shoebox. And the porch, for all its silence, listened like an old friend.

***

Janelle stared at the paper. Seeing the printed announcement delivered finality in a way that the parade and the prior days' activities didn't. She traced his name with her finger, the serif letters sharp against the soft page.

# OBITUARY

Justice Edgar Goodman b. 1925 ✳ – d. 2003 †

Home Builder, Veteran, and Community Pillar

Oakwood, OH. Justice Edgar Goodman, beloved husband, father, army veteran, and founder of Goodman Homes, passed away peacefully on June 18, 2003, at the Veterans Administration Medical Center in Dayton. He was 78 years old.

A veteran of the Korean War and lifelong resident of Montgomery County, Mr. Goodman returned from service with a vision to build homes and communities. After working at General Motors and Hamilton Homes, he launched his construction firm in 1960, developing neighborhoods across Dayton and providing dignified housing to working-class families. He later became known for his craftsmanship, quiet mentorship, and compassion, offering second chances to young men needing direction.

Mr. Goodman's signature yellow Dodge D100 truck and his presence on the front porch became fixtures in the Oakwood community, where neighbors often stopped by for a story, advice, or simply the comfort of his company. In 1985, he retired from construction but continued to manage rental properties and remained active in local restoration efforts.

A dedicated civic leader, he served on numerous community boards, including the Sisters of Charity and the Field and Farm

Discount Chain, a family business he helped steward for over thirty years before its sale to new ownership.

He is survived by his devoted wife, Olive Goodman; his daughter, Janelle Goodman, and her fiancé, Julien Boudreaux; his brother, Reverend Judge (Red) Goodman, (Mildred); along with other nieces and nephews; close family friend Cayenne Boudreaux; and a community that mourns his loss while celebrating his legacy. In honor of his contributions, the City of Oakwood proclaimed June 18, 2003, Justice Goodman Day.

A memorial service will be held at Solidarity Methodist Church on Saturday, June 25, at 11:00 a.m. Instead of flowers, the family requests that donations be made to a local veteran outreach program or a youth mentorship program in his name.

# FIFTEEN

# OAKWOOD KNEW A GOOD MAN

June 25, 2003

THE PORCH HAD known it well. Solidarity Methodist sat at the corner of Third and Main like a sentinel, quiet, worn, and steady. Not because it's wood ever graced the sanctuary or rested beneath the glow of stained glass, but because its parishioners had. And wherever they went, they carried its rhythm with them.

The church stood in grandeur, steeped in memory, in

baptisms and bells, in struggle and sacred song. Far across town, the porch, felt the weight of their footfalls like echoes. They had mourned here before. They would mourn again.

The building is illuminated by the stories shared within its walls of stained glass, limestone and marble, and the footsteps of mourners, mothers, preachers, and elders, and by a community that gathers out of a sense of belonging rather than duty. It held fast in the 1950s and 60s when highways threatened neighborhoods and storefronts gave way to parking lots; the church did not fall. It opened its doors wider. Now, once again, the porch bore witness to Solidarity carrying a people. Justice Goodman would be memorialized here, not just as a man laid to rest, but as a man lifted up.

At the front of the sanctuary, his wife Olive, daughter Janelle, and soon-to-be son-in-law Julien sat with the straight backs of those holding too much. Reverend Judge Goodman, just "Red" to most who knew him, would deliver the eulogy. They came early. Politicians with folded hands. Ballplayers with bowed heads. Neighbors. Elders. Boys who once needed guiding and mothers who remembered when Justice had carried their burdens alongside his own.

The porch had seen many of them on its steps at one time or another. It remembered when Janelle ran barefoot across its floorboards, and when Olive stood silent on summer nights, waiting for headlights in the driveway.

The porch recognized Justice's circle, not always a conventional bunch. Some of his acquaintances might've drawn side-eyes or chuckles, but that never bothered Justice. Kaleb was present, neat as a pin and twice as proud. Oakwood knew him and his Sunday ritual, laying out his suede Stacy Adams on the driveway pavers and washing them with a garden hose. No one understood it, but Kaleb said it kept the nap soft and the spirit clean.

Penny was also present. Oakwood knew her, the town's unofficial herald. She wasn't technically a gossip, she'd say. She just had 'excellent recall.' If she was within earshot, folks on the porch knew to tuck their business in tight or risk hearing it revised and repeated on the prayer line by morning.

And Edgar was stationed in a pew near the front of the church, dear Edgar, loyal to the bone but allergic to hurrying. Oakwood knew him, too. He toted a dented bucket full of tools, though nobody had ever seen him use them. Most days, he sat behind the wheel of the yellow D100, door open, elbow resting, waiting for Justice like a co-pilot in a never-ending workday sitcom. These were Justice's people. Ordinary, peculiar, beloved.

As congregants entered the vestibule to pay their respects, they couldn't help but pause in reverence at the aroma rising like prayer from the fellowship hall below. The air was dense with sustenance. Freshly baked bread, smoky meats, and crispy fried chicken mingled with the slow heat of Cayenne's Cajun spices. It smelled of comfort and homegoing, and *we've got you* in edible form. It wrapped around them, softening grief's edges, pulling up laughter from somewhere deep.

For many, it brought back Justice's porch gatherings, the Fourth of Julys with Cayenne's gumbo simmering, after Sunday service when folks lingered too long because there was always another plate to fix and another story to hear.

Inside, the atmosphere shifted. Warm light filtered through stained glass, casting hues of violet, ruby, and gold across polished pews and the worn hymnals tucked behind each one. The church felt alive, steady, and spacious, like it had been waiting for this.

The choir's voice heralded like angels. Praise hymns wove through the arches, first from the Hammond organ, then from the voices of the choir loft. A single soprano voice rose in the offering, trembled, then steadied as altos, tenors, and basses wrapped around it in solemn harmony.

The porch could not sing, but it had heard the harmonies a thousand times before. People swayed. Some hummed along. Others dabbed their cheeks, lifted a hand, or just bowed their heads. There were no elaborate decorations, lilies, or sprays. In place of flowers, the family requested donations to local veteran outreach or youth mentorship programs in his name. Solidarity was dressed in reminiscence. And the service began.

Reverend Red stood in the pulpit wearing his regalia. He looked regal, like a prince, and humble, like a son, a brother, and a solitary man. "Grace and peace to you, church. Olive, Janelle, and family. Justice has been returned to the earth and is not present here, but his spirit is felt among us." His voice seemed to tremble.

The porch pictured him on his parents' veranda, there, once a boy shouting at his brother from the front steps, now a man trying to lift his brother into eternity. "Look at you, all your faces offer me a glimpse of the life he lived, not left behind because his spirit resides in you."

He reviewed the order of service, read off the song selections from the choir, a soloist, and remarks from those close to Justice, after which he would deliver the eulogy. "Justice was a remarkable man, defined not just by his actions but by his character. Although not overtly religious, he was, in essence, a man of God. Much has been written in your programs, so I won't take up your time by reading it out loud. And, before the others' step forward, I just wanted to say that my brother lived with unwavering determination and resilience even when faced with insurmountable challenges. He loved his family, especially his wife, who, as he often joked, was as tough to win over as a cat in a bathtub."

The church chuckled at this, and Red smiled with a sheepish nod. "Once he convinced her to stick around," he added, "he was as devoted as a dog with a bone. Right?" He turned to Olive with a warm, knowing glance.

A few murmured affirmations fluttered through the pews. Someone called out, "Preach, Rev!"

Red continued. "He would bend over backward for his daughter, not just because she occasionally needed money to go to Westown Mall," he teased, drawing more laughter. "But because she was the darling in his universe."

"Mmhm," someone hummed from the choir section.

"He was always present, ready to cheer her on."

The congregation swayed in gentle agreement. Heads nodded. Hands clutched tissues.

"Now," Red said, softening, "I invite others close to him to share their thoughts. Kindly keep your comments to two minutes. Thank you."

A small group stepped forward in silent formation. Dressed in a crisp button-down and polished shoes, Ronny Black took the mic first. He grinned sheepishly. "I met Mr. Goodman at McDonald's. I was acting tough, flexin,' trying to impress the wrong crowd. He stared me down as if looking through a dirty window and asked, 'What you doing with all that fake fire in your chest?" The crowd laughed. "That man didn't just call me out; he called me up. I went to jail a few months later. And you know what? He wrote me, put money on my books, and said, 'You're better than your worst day.' Who does that? Goodman did."

Next was Loretta McGhee, her voice trembling with gratitude. "I am a single mom of two, living paycheck to paycheck. When I started getting help from the Sisters of Charity, I didn't know Justice had anything to do with it. Then, one day, I showed up to tour the transitional housing and saw him there, wearing a hard hat, a toolbelt, and a smile. 'Come see your future,'" he said. "Goodman built hope."

Bette Day steadied herself with a cane as she approached the podium. She felt for the microphone and leaned forward almost as if keeping time. "I met Justice in Korea. I was a WAC working in the mess hall. One day, I caught a grease fire that left me blind. Years later, when I had nowhere to go, he gave me a patch of land to park my double wide. He looked after me like a brother. Even told me to stop cooking and brought me hot meals so I wouldn't burn the place down. That's love, that's Goodman for you."

Then Cayenne took the mic, regal, dressed in a fuchsia pantsuit and a long yellow silk jacket. "Justice was my brother, by another mother. When I told him I wanted to open a restaurant on the East Side, he didn't blink, just handed me a check. Said, 'Start the fire, Cayenne. I'll bring the bricks.' He never asked for the money back. He just wanted to see me succeed. He showed up again, with lined pockets, when it came time to expand the existing space." Her words caught in her throat, and she let the tears spill. "I am going to miss my brother," and she turned to take her seat.

Justice's niece and nephew stepped forward. Clarice's voice cracked as she began, "Uncle Justice made sure we never missed a Christmas, a family dinner, or a backyard barbecue. Horace II added that even after our father died, and our mom got sick and had to go into the nursing home, Unc never let us feel forgotten. He made sure our lives remained full of love."

A few wandering chords from the Hammond organ filled a brief pause, the kind of unscripted interlude Solidarity knew by heart. Finally, the mayor approached the podium with a warm smile lighting up his face.

"Greetings from the office of the mayor!" he announced, his voice carrying authority and charm. "The mayor's office has set this day, June 18, 2003, as Justice Goodman Day in Dayton."

The porch bore witness, not for titles or seals, but for the truth embedded in the words.

"CITY OF DAYTON MAYORAL PROCLAMATION IN HONOR OF MR. JUSTICE GOODMAN.

WHEREAS, the City of Dayton acknowledges the passing of a treasured citizen, Justice Goodman, who devoted his life to family, community, and the betterment of others.

WHEREAS, Mr. Goodman was a Korean War veteran, a skilled tradesman, the founder of Goodman Homes, and a steadfast pillar in the Oakwood community for more than six decades.

WHEREAS his vision and craftsmanship contributed to the development and preservation of neighborhoods across Dayton, and his quiet leadership and acts of service uplifted neighbors, newcomers, and friends.

WHEREAS Mr. Goodman was known not only for his integrity and work ethic but also for the kindness he extended without fanfare, the wisdom he shared on porches and at community gatherings, and the deep love he carried for his wife, Olive, daughter Janelle, and extended family.

NOW, THEREFORE, BE IT RESOLVED that I, Harold

Monroe, Mayor of the City of Dayton, do hereby proclaim that: June 25, 2003, shall be known as Justice Goodman Day throughout the City of Dayton.

On this day, we pause to remember a man who left footprints not only in concrete but also in the hearts of all who knew him. We honor his memory and commit to carrying forward his legacy of dignity, humility, and service.

IN WITNESS WHEREOF, I hereunto set my hand and cause the Seal of the City of Dayton to be affixed this 25th day of June 2003. Frank Monroe, Mayor of Dayton."

The congregation clapped and responded with hearty amens, sniffles, and knowing glances. Justice Goodman had left fingerprints on every heart in the room. Red stepped forward again. "Thank you all. Justice didn't just live in this city; he helped build it. And he made room for all of us to grow inside it. Amen? Come on, choir, let's praise the Lord."

The choir stood and launched into a soul-stirring rendition of Going Up Yonder, harmonies washing through the sanctuary and lifting spirits skyward. After the musical selection, a slight movement from the rear of the sanctuary drew everyone's attention. Eva Du Bois stood from a pew in the back and slowly walked toward the podium.

The porch had known that face for decades–hardened, trembling, then suddenly soft when she looked at Janelle. A murmuring ripple spread across the congregation. Red hesitated. Cayenne's lips parted in concern. Olive looked down. Janelle's eyes widened.

Eva reached the front, her black shift swaying just above her ballet slippers, gold hoops catching a flicker of light. Her hair was swept into a bun, her face bare of makeup but etched with raw emotion. She looked directly at Janelle. "Justice helped me… when I had a baby out of wedlock," she said.

The room quieted. Her voice didn't falter, though her eyes glistened. "He didn't judge me like some of y'all did. Didn't turn his nose up when I came through. Didn't cast his vote to get me kicked outta church fellowship or whisper behind my back like my sin might spread like fire. Nah, he saw me. He saw me."

The porch, though miles away, had seen this pain before. Countless nights. Front steps dances and breakdowns. Eva watches Janelle play, watches Olive cook, watches a life that might have been hers, but never tries to take it.

Eva turned slightly toward the congregation, her gaze sweeping over the rows like a wind bending tall grass. "He saw me when I was full of the poison, wearing that too-big, dirty overcoat, the one I used to hide my shame. Y'all remember? I wore it in the heat of summer. Heat couldn't shame me more than my own skin." She took a breath, slower now. "He didn't exile me to my low-rent apartment in DeSota Bass, tucked away from the neat rows and clean lawns of Oakwood. Didn't act like my mistakes might stain his porch. He let me sit right there. On his porch. Where truth and grace met me every time."

A murmur stirred in the pews, some shifting in discomfort, others leaning forward. Eva's eyes narrowed, voice tightening. "He didn't kick me off that porch to make y'all feel more at ease. So don't pretend now like you forgot how you looked at me, and some of y'all called me 'crazy.' Like, grace is selective. Justice didn't turn his back. He gave me a place to breathe." Then, more softly, to Janelle again. "He gave me hope when I didn't think I deserved it. That's the kind of man your father was."

The air was filled with whispers. Red's knuckles turned white as they gripped the pulpit. Cayenne became rigid. Olive closed her eyes and fiddled with her wedding ring.

Eva tried to continue, but her voice cracked. Her lips trembled. "Nope. No. He, he didn't judge me," she whispered. Tears streamed down her cheeks. The porch witnessed her pain many times over. She was always watching, especially the movements of Janelle Goodman. She paused. An usher gently stepped forward and stood beside her. Janelle moved, too, crossing the sanctuary to meet them. Eva could no longer speak. She buried her face in her hands. Quietly and respectfully, the usher and Janelle led her out of the sanctuary to a quiet room. The porch didn't need to follow; it had already seen what mattered.

Red cleared his throat. "Let us pray for Miss Du Bois," he said. "For healing, for peace, and understanding."

The congregation responded softly with an "Amen."

Red took a breath, hands gripping the pulpit as he steadied himself. "My brother was a good man," he began, voice soft but resolute. "Not perfect. Not always easy. But he was steady. He was present. And he was generous in ways most folks never knew."

He continued with an honest and heartfelt tribute, speaking of Justice's fierce loyalty, flaws, laughter, and quiet service to others. When he concluded, Red wiped his brow and raised his hand. "Now, may the grace of God, the love of Jesus, and the fellowship of the Holy Spirit be with us all. Join us in the fellowship hall for the repast." He closed the service, like the pulpit might catch fire if he lingered too long, or worse, someone might stand up and say something that would turn him into a pillar of salt.

And far from the sanctuary, the porch sat still. It didn't shift or creak or speak. But it knew. Some truths have waited lifetimes to surface. And others, like smoke rising when the fire is finally out.

***

The atmosphere in the fellowship hall pulsed with emotion. Joy and sorrow, hope and grief. Laughter punctuated soft sobs, and hugs lingered a second too long. Janelle, flanked by her mother, Mildred, and Cayenne, welcomed guests as they filtered in with prayers and condolences. Nearby, Julien reappeared from the dessert table, balancing three bowls of bread pudding and a towering slice of red velvet cake. Just as he passed Cayenne her dish, Red approached.

"Julien, may I speak with you? Just a few minutes upstairs in the study."

"Now?" Julien snapped, his voice sharper than he meant.

Marcus hovered over Fern and Janelle, too close for comfort, and his patience wore thin. "Can't this wait?"

"Yes, now please," Red said, eyes darting nervously.

Julien exhaled deeply, handed off the dessert, squeezed Janelle's hand, and said, "I'll be right back," then trudged up the stairs, the weight of the day pressing on his shoulders. Cayenne watched him go, a plate still in her hand, the red velvet slice sliding slightly to one side, something in her stilled. Julien's voice, the way his shoulders tensed, when the gaps between him and his father tried to close, and he didn't know how to handle it. Cayenne set the dessert down and followed.

Julien flung open the door to the study. "Nice setup, Dad. Got the reverend suite just the way you like it, huh?"

At the top of the stairs, Cayenne didn't knock. She stood just outside the study door, close enough to hear when the storm broke, far enough to give him room to weather it. She had seen too many reckonings happen behind closed doors. This time, she would be close.

Inside, Red clasped his hands and bowed his head in a brief prayer. He knew he needed help. "Holy Spirit, I need you." He stood there not as a person of the cloth but as a humble man seeking redemption.

Julien raised a brow. "You did a nice job eulogizing Unc today. I was impressed. Thanks for that."

"Son, I've led this congregation like a shepherd. But I've also strayed like a restless sheep. And I've hidden in the shadows."

Julien folded his arms. "Is this about to turn into a sermon?"

Red's eyes dropped to the floor. "After Korea, I came back and tried to build something with your mother. It didn't last. You were already on the way. I felt the call to ministry, but Cayenne wasn't on that path. We split. I joined Solidarity. Married Mildred."

"I know all that," Julien said, his voice layered with a mixture of impatience and long-harbored resentment. "I know about your calling. I know about how you chose the church, and how you chose her. What you gave up is what was left behind. Mom never depended on you for money, for security, just for something as basic as a father showing up. And she didn't get that. That's why I stayed here instead of attending graduate school out of state. I built my life and career here. To give her what you couldn't. To help with the restaurant, to make sure she had stability, even though she'd never ask for it. I didn't leave because someone had to be here, and that someone wasn't you." Julien's jaw tightened, the old bitterness simmering just beneath his words. "You went where you were called. I stayed where I was needed."

For a moment, Red's gaze flicked upward, as if he were about to say something, an apology, a justification. But the words landed in the drought of his voice box. His shoulders sagged slightly, as if admitting defeat in the face of his son's truth. And then, almost as if escaping his shame, his voice dropped to a whisper. "I cheated on Mildred with Eva DuBois."

Julien blinked. "Wait. You're Eva's baby daddy!"

A suffocating silence filled the room.

Red gave a solemn nod.

"No. No. No!" Julien's voice cracked. "Dad, seriously? I asked the question as a joke. Holy shit. I didn't mean, Crazy Eva? That woman? I didn't know she had your baby! I was stunned when she stood up today. Is it a boy or a girl?"

Red didn't flinch; he was compelled by something greater than himself. "Janelle is mine and Eva's baby."

Julien staggered backward. "Nah… No, no, no! Uncle Justice and Olive are her parents. We're cousins!"

"You're siblings," Red said, his voice steady but heavy as if the weight of the truth hung between them.

The fury exploded. Julien's fists clenched, his face contorted. "You son of a bitch! You lied to me my whole life? She doesn't even know, does she? Oh God! Janelle doesn't know!"

"Julien…"

"I've got to get the hell out of here." He burst through the door, almost crashing into his mother, who stood outside with nervous anticipation.

"Julien, wait!" Cayenne called after him, but he was already storming out of the church. Cayenne felt lost, unable to determine her next move. Julien passed Eva outside the church, a cigarette trembling between her fingers. Her eyes met his, searching for something. He shoved past her without a word.

A couple of friends called out as he passed. "Hey man, see you at the wedding!"

"You and Janelle make a lovely couple."

Julien didn't respond. The words followed him into the growing dusk like echoes from a collapsing world.

Red stood motionless in his study as the tears rolled down his face. Yet his posture spoke of a heavy burden, free of the haunting ghosts from the past. Mildred appeared, making her way from the fellowship hall, and walked past Cayenne with quiet resolve. Her stride was steady, unbothered by uncertainty. She knew what her husband needed, and she was the only one who could answer that call.

She paused briefly outside the vestry door, then knocked once and entered, carrying a pot of coffee and two mugs. "I brought cof," she paused, taking in the expression on her husband's face. She moved toward him with the determination of a warrior confronting darkness and wrapped her arms around him tightly. She whispered in his ear, "Judge, we are now at the mercy seat. The whole truth is out; I am proud of you."

After witnessing the scene, Cayenne returned to the fellowship hall, feeling the weight of Red's revelation. As congregants began to leave, Olive spotted her unease. "Cayenne, you ready to leave? I think we're done here." Studying her friend, she asked. "What's the matter, sweetie? You, okay?"

Cayenne's gaze was unwavering yet troubled. She replied bluntly, "Julien knows about Red and Eva. The truth is out."

Olive gently placed her hands on her friend's shoulders, her voice steady yet full of warmth as she said, "Baby, God knows the beginning and the end of this story. We're gonna walk through this fire together. I trust Him, not only for what He has done but also for who He is."

Cayenne nodded in agreement. Together, they held up each other, their hearts intertwined as they walked toward the exit, feeling the weight of the moment between them.

In what seemed like a synchronized moment, Janelle and Fern approached the women, their expressions filled with curiosity. Janelle spoke. "I was looking for Julien to bring the car around. Where is he? Does anyone know?"

# PART TWO

*No one was truly alone as long as the porch held space for them.*

# SIXTEEN

# BALM IN PINEVIEW

THE ANGEL OAK dappled a shadow on the sun-warmed walls of Olive's bedroom. The Cuisinart growled to life in the kitchen, grinding coffee beans into a familiar whir, followed by the soft trickle of brewing. The scent of hazelnut lifted like incense and drifted through the quiet house.

Olive swung her old lady legs over the bed, her knees resisting movement, and slipped into her worn slippers. She padded past Janelle's bedroom, where a soft snore and the shape of tucked-in feet poked out from beneath a mountain of blankets.

On a typical morning, she would've filled her mug, crossed

the porch's stretch of wood, and found Justice already there, elbows on the rail, second cup in hand, offering a story, a grumble, or a knowing silence. But today, only heartache waited. Olive gripped the edges of the counter as she poured her coffee, seeking steadiness. She needed something-or someone-to steady her Spirit.

*Miss Lilly.*

The name rose like a balm. The one who took her in after her grandfather's death, who ran that big house in Pineview like it was a temple and a refuge. She'd given Olive more than a roof. She'd given her dignity. Now, Miss Lilly lies in a hospice. Her bones were failing, but her mind remained as sharp as a wood-splitting axe. Olive didn't tell anyone where she was going. She didn't have time.

The Buick LeSabre whirred to life, the weight of time embedded in its frame. Olive drove with quiet focus, knuckles pale against the wheel. Pineview rolled toward her, a quilt of red brick roads and pine-laden skies. Old mailboxes leaned like weary sentinels set against golden fields.

She turned onto a gravel drive that crunched under the tires. The residence stood at the end, its white paint weathered, a couple shutters ajar, the wraparound porch still clinging to its dignity. A familiar hush fell over her as she stepped inside like a blanket warmed on a line.

It smelled of lemon balm, old wood, and lavender salve. A nurse offered a soft nod and pointed toward the private wing. Olive walked past a row of quiet rooms. In one of them, she observed a worn Bible on a nightstand, a silk scarf folded neatly beside it. As she passed another, she heard the melodic ornamentation of Mahalia Jackson's contralto voice echo throughout the hallways. She reached Miss Lilly's suite, paused, and tiptoed inside.

Miss Lilly's living room was a museum of memory and meaning, each wall curated with purpose. Framed photos lined the plaster like scripture, black-and-white snapshots of groundbreaking ceremonies, posed dinners with city notables, a young Miss Lilly standing proud beside her husband as they surveyed the construction of new dorms. But it was one photo, nestled near the bookcase, that caught Olive's breath.

There she was, young, uncertain, yet beaming, standing beneath the frescoed ceiling in Miss Lilly's ornate library, her arms stacked high with borrowed books, Miss Lilly beside her, hand resting firm on Olive's shoulder. That smile… Lord, she hadn't seen that version of herself in years. It was the grin of a girl who, for the first time in a long time, had believed she was going somewhere.

 Lillian Pierre, the proprietor of Pierre Place for Women and Girls, communicated with the edge of a woman who'd learned early not to waste words. Her sharpness wasn't cruelty. It was precision. She had honed it alongside her late husband, a prominent attorney in Dayton. An Irishman who made his fortune defending lawbreakers and troublemakers. He wasn't a man guided by moral outcomes. He

cared more for the strategy, the spectacle, and the fees that followed. But there was one thing he truly cared about, Lillian Pierre.

Miss Lilly.

Miss Lilly once told Olive that in Ireland, a groom was expected to present his bride with a ring. But her Irish husband had gone another way, placing a deed in her hand instead. By then, the courtroom theater had soured her. She had seen enough guilty men go free and enough broken women left without a voice.

She'd taken that patch of land and, with stubborn grace, turned it into a home for girls, a gift remade into something neither love nor law could take away. It was a crumbling, echo-filled place with vines creeping up the wooden and brick structure, featuring chipped cherubs in the garden set among acres of a heavily wooded landscape. Lilly walked its halls once and saw not ruin, but refuge.

The halls of Miss Lilly's weren't just walls and windows. They echoed with late-night laughter, whispered confessions, the clatter of hot combs on stove burners, and the sizzling of grease as the heated metal pulled through curly hair, and the quiet resolve of girls who had been forced to start over.

Some came in angry, traumatized, and hardened. Most hadn't come with dreams, only needs. But over time, with Miss Lilly's questions and firm hands, those needs began to shape into a vision.

Olive arrived at Pierre Place bruised by betrayal and nearly penniless. Miss Lilly took her in without a sermon, without pity, just structure, space, and the kind of stillness where a woman could learn to breathe again. Miss Lilly loved sharply and gave freely. She offered shelter, not promises. Boundaries, not blame. For Olive, it was enough. For a while, it was everything. "What do you want to be, Olive?" she asked one evening, her apron styled around her middle, covering an elegant shift, as the girls set the table for dinner.

Olive had answered like her Pops' bones and marrow had quickened inside her. "I want to own something. Build something. I want to be a teacher."

Miss Lilly nodded once, approval sharp as her tongue. "Then you'd best get to the library. Can't build anything real if you don't know what's possible."

That was Miss Lilly. No empty praise. No false hope. Just hard truths, honest work, and the belief that love, real love-was found in consistency, in showing up, in helping a girl stand taller than she arrived. Through books, Olive learned about a world bigger than herself and how she fit in it. From Miss Lilly, she learned to recognize her value, name her vision, and walk it out, step by step.

***

Miss Lilly lay in her hospital bed, her eyes closed, but her breathing slow and even. Her silver hair was wrapped in a floral scarf; her hands rested atop a hand-stitched quilt that looked like it was sewn perhaps by one of the girls she'd raised. The

138

room glowed with filtered light sprinkled through lace curtains.

"Miss Lilly, it's Olive." She whispered, settling into the chair beside her, cradling her coffee like a shield. "I came to talk. I have a lot on my mind, so much I want to say."

The old woman's eyes fluttered open. They were still bright, still wise. And they saw right through her.

"Then talk," she rasped, voice thin but rooted. "I ain't gone yet."

"Justice is gone, Miss Lilly."

"Gone. Where child?"

Olive's voice trembled. "He said he was going ahead to check on your mansion in heaven. Said he needed to make sure the good Lord had everything under control."

Miss Lilly's lips curled faintly. "That boy. I didn't tell him to do that. He gon' before me?"

"Yes, ma'am."

Miss Lilly let out a long sigh. "When I get there, I'm gon whip his backside. Leaving you down here like this."

Olive smiled weakly, but the smile faltered. "Miss Lilly, I'm about to break our baby's heart. How do I tell her the truth we've held on to for so long? We always planned to tell her about the adoption. Were we wrong for not telling her sooner?" She shrugged. "We thought their affection would pass. They broke up before. We told ourselves cousins would be fine. But siblings?" She paused, the weight of the truth unbearable. "It's not biblical, Miss Lilly. It's dangerous. It's wrong. God opened and closed that gene code long ago. They can't, they can't. I don't even know where to begin."

Miss Lilly opened her eyes wider, sharp and steady. "Baby, there ain't no perfect way to tell her. We are a work in progress, at war with perfection and imperfection. And we don't blame ourselves, and we sho' don't blame the baby. Sometimes, it's through heartbreak that beautiful things are made." She reached out a fragile hand. "Now, help me sit up. I've still got a little breath left for wisdom."

Olive guided her gently. Once upright, Miss Lilly adjusted the scarf on her head and fixed Olive with a look that cut through fear and shame. "Olive, you raised a smart girl. She already has questions bubbling under the surface, she don't know how to ask 'em, 'cause she don't want to hurt nobody, and she don't want to let go of that boy. Julien, that's his name, right? That boy cares for your baby. There's safety in that love. She left Dayton, trying to find herself, and then found her way back to him. That returning, that's not accidental."

"She doesn't trust herself to start over," Olive murmured.

"She don't need to. She knows him. Their friendship is pure, mixed with eros. Agape? That comes after a storm. That's the kind of love that survives fire. And it might be stronger if they love each other outside the bonds of marriage."

Olive's eyes filled, lips trembling.

"You don't need a lecture," Miss Lilly said bluntly. "You'll muster the courage, and you can start by forgiving Justice for what he didn't say, and for leaving you to carry what should've been shared. Let go of that angst, baby. It'll be the death of you. Speak from your heart. The Spirit will do the rest."

Miss Lilly leaned back and sucked on her lips. "Can you hand me some water, baby?"

Olive rose slowly and crossed the room to pour a glass from the pitcher.

When she turned back, the light had changed. Miss Lilly was still. Gone.

She had left the room the way only saints do, as if she had an appointment to keep. No parting words. No drawn-out goodbye. Just a quiet exhale, and a knowing. She and God had already planned her last assignment. And she had fulfilled it.

Olive pressed the nurse's call button with trembling fingers. She pulled the covers up gently, smoothing them with care. Then, she took Miss Lilly's hand and patted it twice, like always when words wouldn't come.

The staff entered quietly, their eyes scanning but their mouths still. They knew. Before Olive turned to leave, she leaned in close and whispered. "Rest now. You've done your part." Then she stood tall, turned toward the door, and walked out to face what came next.

The Buick LeSabre rolled slowly out of the gravel drive, its tires crunching with an oddly reverent rhythm. Olive sat behind the wheel, one hand resting at noon, the other pressed gently over her heart like a lid on a simmering pot. The sun had shifted in the west, casting long gold bands across the pines, the same ones that had whispered over her during the drive-in, but now, they murmured something different.

She didn't turn on the radio. The silence held her like a hymn. The quiet settled into the marrow, not empty but full of memory, regret, and the holy mystery that comes only after loss. The road home curved like an old river.

Every field she passed, every tired barn and leaning post felt like it bowed in mourning for Miss Lilly. That woman had poured herself into so many. Into Olive. And now her hands were still. Olive blinked away a tear. She didn't want to cry too hard, not on the road. But the ache throbbed behind her ribs, and every mile felt like another page turning in a book she wasn't ready to finish.

At a stoplight on Lakeview, she glanced over at the passenger seat, half-expecting to see Miss Lilly, wrapped in a shawl, commenting on the weather or asking why Olive insisted on living in her own house, separate from Justice. "Just ain't normal," she would shake her head and say. The phantom warmth of her voice made Olive press a hand to her mouth.

The light turned green. She drove on. She didn't know what she was going to say to Janelle. She just knew it had to be soon. The truth was now a living thing that would not be buried.

When Olive returned from Pineview, the shadows on Liberty Lane had lengthened, stretching across the porch like fingers trying to hold onto the day. Janelle stood at the top step, her BlackBerry pressed tightly to her ear, as she paced. Her brows were furrowed, her voice sharp and rising. "Stanley, I need the final proof of the Cordel Zane media package by noon tomorrow, not Friday. If Pittsburgh wants it by kickoff, we move. No excuses."

"We have a compelling storyline. Zane, a walk-on, the ultimate underdog, has defied the odds to seize the starting QB position! He lights up the field with relentless determination and incredible skill, proving that hard work pays off. His rise is nothing short of legendary, inspiring teammates and fans to believe in their dreams. This is more than just a game; it's a thrilling tale of triumph that everyone will be talking about! And loop me in on that licensing hiccup immediately." Her tone was definitive.

Olive parked the Buick slowly, her eyes narrowing at the tension wrapped around her daughter like a too-tight blazer. She watched as Janelle ended the call, reassuring Stanley, who was shouldering the mantle like a rock star. "You got this," she said before exhaling and waving her mother up with a whirl of her hand. "I need to talk," Janelle said. Her voice was a mixture of urgency and something close to unraveling.

"Of course," Olive replied softly, climbing the steps.

Janelle blurted before Olive could fully settle beside her. "I haven't heard from Julien since the service yesterday. Not a text. Not a call. Nothing. You know how we are, Mom. We don't go that long. It's weird."

Olive steadied herself. "I think I heard from Cayenne that he and his dad had words. Maybe he needed some breathing space. Everything is happening all at once."

Janelle nodded quickly, but her eyes darted, unfocused. "Maybe. But I was supposed to finalize the menu with him this morning and review the seating chart tonight. Additionally, I would like to return to Chicago to meet with my team. I need to tie up loose ends, have my last fitting, and pack for the wedding and honeymoon."

Olive placed a gentle hand on Janelle's arm. "Do you have a few minutes to walk over to the barn? I haven't seen the decorations yet, and I'd like to talk. Just the two of us."

Janelle hesitated; her BlackBerry was still clutched like a lifeline. Then she sighed, nodded, and tucked it into her bag. "Sure. Okay. I'm so sorry, I'm distracted, but I'm here for you, Mom. Do you need assistance with any aspect of the Trust paperwork? I can arrange a meeting with the lawyer?"

Olive drew in a slow, steady breath. "No, baby. There's nothing urgent I need to do for that now." She extended her hand, the way she had so many times before. Janelle's fingers slipped into her palm, smaller once, now grown, but the weight of them still carried the same pull. Olive closed her hand around her daughter's, guiding her forward, unsure if the path ahead held comfort or trouble, only knowing it wasn't time to let go.

They stepped off the porch and into the shimmering light, crossing the yard where laughter had once echoed. Summer chairs still faced the empty space where Justice used to hold court. As they approached the barn, the air thickened with silence, heavy with everything yet to be said.

145

# SEVENTEEN

# UNRAVELING THE MIRACLE

THE SUNLIGHT PEEKED through the barn rafters casting a warm, hearth-like glow inside the barn. It felt sacred. Janelle, hand in hand with her mother, navigated through the sawdust and scattered lumber, making their way to the bench in front of the large, beamed arch built with hands they loved.

Janelle cleared space for Olive to sit first, her hand brushing along the edge of the bench like she needed grounding. "Your father took such care with this build-out," she said, her voice heavy with emotion. "He wanted to create something that would outlast pain and turn distress into something beautiful."

Janelle tilted her head, puzzled. "Pain?"

Olive looked straight ahead, her voice soft. "We were worried about keeping something from you. But your father…he loved you more than he feared the truth."

Janelle's shoulders stiffened. "Mom, your words, your tone, you're scaring me."

"We never meant to keep it forever. We intended to tell you. We were waiting for the right moment, but it kept eluding us. Justice was torn, baby. So, he did the only thing he knew how to do when his heart was heavy– he built. He painted, stained, and sanded through the guilt. The barn was his apology and his blessing. Your Dad was always making offerings, as if he wasn't enough. He wanted to give you something beautiful. Something that said, '*you* were worth building for.' But the wedding to Julien made time run out. It created an urgency we couldn't outrun."

Janelle took a breath. "Because we're cousins? Mom, we worked through that. It's not customary by some standards, but we…"

"Janelle," Olive interrupted, gently but firmly. "Your father suffered a traumatic injury in Korea. We tried for years to have a child on our own. Then, you came. You were our miracle. Maybe not in the way we expected, but God heard us. And He answered."

Janelle sat frozen, every muscle tight, her mind racing.

"We fostered children. We loved one boy as if he were ours. When he was placed with another family, it shattered us. After that, we decided that the next child who came to our home would stay. When the call came, they said, 'We have a baby. She's a good match for you. Would you foster her? I said yes before the woman could finish."

Olive reached into her bag and pulled out the envelopes, one a letter and the other an adoption birth certificate. "You were that baby. We adopted you. Your father wrote this letter for you. We always meant to give it to you at the right time. But it can't wait any longer."

Tears welled in Janelle's eyes. "Oh, Mom." Janelle's jaw stiffened, eyes fixed and unblinking, as if her mind had jammed on a thought too heavy to move. "I don't know why. It's like part of me already knew. It explains so much. At the pediatrician, when you didn't have all the answers, when I'd search your face for mine and only sometimes find it. I convinced myself that I had inherited Dad's features, so his genes must've been stronger. That's what I told myself. And lately, you've both seemed haunted. I thought it was because Julien and I are cousins, and you two and the family felt it was taboo. But we're not, are we? We're not actually cousins, not by blood at least."

Janelle bowed over in laughter, incredulous and relieved. "We're not related! Not by blood. Oh my God, Mom! Do you know what this means? All those years, there was doubt, and I secretly ran from it for a time, but my wedding to Julien was destined. Mom, this-this is the best wedding gift you could've given me!" Janelle leapt into her mother's arms and hugged her tightly, holding her close. Janelle felt her mother stiffen.

Olive pulled back. "Janelle, baby, I'm sorry."

Janelle's smile faded. "Sorry? Mom, it's ok, it's ok…"

"Baby, listen." Olive now gripping Janelle in the crease of her arms. "Your Uncle Red had a child with another woman while married to Mildred. He and the child's mother decided it was best to place the baby for adoption. They wanted to protect Red's appointment to the clergy, and they didn't think they could raise the child together."

Janelle's face once sparkled a breath ago; now, her face read like a closed door. "Mom? The mother, is it?" Pause, "Eva?"

Olive nodded; the truth was heavy in the air. "Yes, baby. Eva is your biological mother. And Red. Red is your biological father."

Janelle's breath caught in her throat. Her voice dropped to a whisper. "No? No. That would mean... Julien and I…" Her voice cracked.

"You're brother and sister."

Janelle's voice modulated like a skipped heartbeat. "No. No. No. No. NO!" The first few were soft refusals, half disbelief, half pleas. But the last was louder, jagged–tore loose from her chest, final and full of fire. Janelle stumbled backward, her body trembling. The barn suddenly spun, and the rafters swayed with the force of the truth. The wedding arch stood behind them, unwavering, while the world tilted.

# EIGHTEEN

# THE BARN IS BURNING

THE PORCH HAD held joy, and endured grief. But what came next, that silence after a truth explodes, was something different. Not even the cicadas sang. It was the kind of quiet that settles when something breaks open for good.

Janelle ran. Her shoes barely touched the earth between the barn and the cottage, her palazzo pants trailing like a banner of surrender. The porch felt her before it saw her, felt the rush of confusion, the fury, the wild rhythm of a woman undone.

She stumbled on the top step and caught the rail like a lifeline. Then she disappeared inside. But the porch didn't release her. It listened as her body crumpled onto the love seat, as grief hissed through her teeth. It felt her reach for the photo frame, and it trembled in her hands, and the way her voice cracked around the words she never saw coming. *Brother and sister... me and Julien?*

The photograph showed her and Julien in front of the oak tree last spring. His arms were around her, their foreheads touching. The picture now echoed a sin neither of them knew they'd made. She clutched it, stared into their smiling faces, and then let out a sound, something primal, the sound of a world splitting down the middle, not a sob, not a scream.

Eva stood by the rail from the porch, ashes from her slow burning cigarette falling to the ground unnoticed. "She knows now," she murmured to no one. Her fingers trembled as she brought the smoke to her lips. She wasn't crying. Not yet. Just hollow.

Eva began to hum, then sing softly and unsteadily, like a lullaby remembered from too long ago. *Big Girls Don't Cry,* she whispered more than sang, the words catching on something tender. She'd sung it once when Janelle was still part of her, cradled in a body carrying more ache than answers. Now, she sang it again, hoping the notes might slip through walls and settle around her girl like a blanket.

Inside the barn, Olive hadn't moved. Her body was still on the bench, but her spirit was elsewhere, chasing her daughter, calling out to Justice, praying to God. Her lips barely moved, but the words came steady. "Help us, Lord. Help us- if you can do anything, and I know you can, you can fix this."

The porch watched. Because that's what it did, it held. It kept. It bore witness. Even when everything else burned. Janelle sat in the room, eerily silent, in her parents' house. She was doing that thing with her hair, pulling strands from her crown, a habit born of deep thought. Her mind spiraled with questions. Where was Julien? Why had her parents kept the truth buried? What does it all mean? What would happen to them now?

That first question answered itself when she looked up and saw Julien standing in front of her, like a warrior preparing for a battle, he knew he couldn't win, carrying only a shield of truth. She looked at him, tears streaming down her face. "Julien, what the hell is happening?" she asked, voice cracking. "My mom told me. It doesn't make sense, for real, is this happening?"

"I know, babe. I found out at the funeral, of all places, and it blindsided me. I needed a minute… no, I needed more than a minute to even breathe through it. I'm sorry for leaving you alone." He sank onto the cushion beside her, his knee bouncing with a nervous energy he couldn't quite hide. He gently pried her fingers from her hair, holding them in his palms like something that might slip away if he loosened his grip.

His voice wavered, then sharpened. "This… this is going to take time to figure out. I love you, Janelle Grace Goodman. God, I've loved you since we were kids." He shook his head, dragging a hand across his face before letting out a humorless laugh. "And now what? They expect me to just… turn it off? Like love's a damn breaker switch? Like this is one of our properties, and the wiring's wrong, so we rip it out, rewrite the code, and, bam, it's fine again?" His jaw clenched, eyes darting toward the floor as if looking for solid ground. "Oh, sure. The girl I've loved my whole life is suddenly my sister, so we can't be married. Just like that." His hands tightened around hers. "What the hell!"

Janelle stiffened. "A shit show is what it is. I don't want to change how I love. I like how we love. I want to be married to you!"

Julien stepped back just enough to see her face. "I know. Me too. But this is the first time I thought about surviving. We always just did, you know? Can we survive this?"

Julien's words rattled in the air between them, heavy with the same stubborn fire that had once drawn her to him. Janelle felt the years peel back, not to this latest revelation, but to another moment when the ground shifted beneath them. Grad school acceptance letters, late-night arguments that bled into dawn, and the quiet understanding that love alone wouldn't bridge the miles.

...somewhere between paper deadlines and permanent decisions

Sunbeams danced through the sheer curtains, casting a vibrant gold hue across Janelle's bohemian artwork, affixed to the studio wall. Tiny dust particles floated in slow motion, graceful, glittering in the sunlight. At the same time, down the hall, a door slammed shut with the familiar, resonant thud of lively college life. The scent of cocoa clung to the studio walls, mingling with the familiar notes of her daily existence, curry from a forgotten takeout container, and faint sandalwood from a burned-out incense cone.

Baking brownies always steadied her nerves, and this was one last time, one final batch in her college apartment, before she packed the mixing bowl for good. Corrugated boxes were towered against the wall like mini skyscrapers. Her diploma, framed and wrapped in bubble wrap, leaned beside a box labeled BOOKS / DO NOT LOSE.

Julien stood near the window, leaning over a shelf, surveying the nearly empty apartment. He looked good, very good. Like six feet of sun-kissed chocolate wrapped in confidence and contradiction, muscles flexing just enough to prove a point without trying. "You did your thing, babe," he said. "You did it. We did it," he sounded proud, but Janelle caught the edge in his voice. "But I still don't get it," he continued. "Why the rush? Why now?"

Janelle, sealing another box, turned away from him. "I need to do this, or I worry I'll wake up at thirty-five, stuck in a life I didn't choose. College gave us some freedom, but it didn't fully free us. We've never been apart since we were kids. I need some distance to find out who I am, apart from you and away from Dayton. It's time for me to take this step for myself."

He stepped toward her, dropping his voice to that tone, the one that always dangerously got under her skin. "You could've renewed the lease. It's just a few more months before grad school starts. We could've stayed here. Figured things out together."

Her hands trembled, she peeled the tape too hard, and it snapped. "It's not about being together, Julien. I'm going to Northwestern. That's the plan." She looked up, steady now. "I'm not like my parents. I can't let love be the whole story. I have to take what they gave me, test it, and build something new." She drew a breath. "If I stay, I'll disappear in us. You'll become the only thing I live for. And I can't do that, not now." She softened, just barely. "I love you, Julien Boudreaux. Deeply. Don't make this harder than it already is."

He was searching for something as if he already knew the answer. "Technically, we are not really cousins, J," he said suddenly. "People act like it's scandalous, but it's not. This won't be the first time cousins in the family married, and it won't be the last."

"We're not cousins, really, since when?" she snapped, her sarcasm slicing through the air like a blade. "Last I checked, a cousin is the child of one's uncle or aunt. And not just any cousin, first cousins. My dad and your father are brothers. We have the same grandparents, Horace Sr. and Beatrice Goodman. Remember them? That's how this works." She punctuated her words with the exasperated precision of someone trapped in a conversation looping endlessly, like a dull, nagging lyric she couldn't turn off.

Julien exhaled, frustrated. "Yeah, but I'm a Boudreaux, not a Goodman. My father split before I was born, didn't even raise me."

"Boy, stop! You can't explain this away just because you got some legitimacy issues going on. Uncle Red is your daddy," she snapped. "Stop it! You graduated summa cum laude in engineering. You're a freaking scientist! I suppose what they say is true: book smarts without common sense." Janelle gave him a silly look, then turned away and back again.

Her voice softened, but the edge was still there. "Honestly, Julien, I don't care what people think. I care what I think. And I chose this. I need to know who I am outside of this city. Outside of you."

Just then, excruciating screams came from the apartment across the hall. They both froze. "What the hell!" Julien yelled.

Janelle opened the door a crack. "That's coming from Fern's place." They rushed into the hallway and knocked on her door. No answer. The moaning continued. The door stood ajar, and Julien reached for the knob. "I'm calling 911," Janelle shrieked.

The moaning stopped. Julien pushed open the door wider this time. Seconds later, Fern's bedroom door opened slightly, and Francis Ikaika, a.k.a Grunt, UD's backup tackle, emerged, shirtless, sweaty, and grinning. "What?" he shrugged.

Fern peeked out from behind him, waving sheepishly.

Julien shook his head. "Man, we thought someone was dying in here."

"Nope. Just living."

Janelle cracked up. It was precisely the release the room needed.

When they stepped back into her apartment, the moment between them softened. Julien rubbed her arms gently. "You sure about this?" he asked.

She nodded. "I am."

He pulled her into a long hug. "Well, it's only a 4-hour drive."

"Then let's make this the part of our story we don't regret."

***

She shook her head; her eyes flooded with tears. "What do you mean, can we survive this? We held a long-distance relationship for years. Did you think I didn't question everything? From graduate school to choosing Chicago over Dayton, my career, dating my cousin, oh, wait, who I thought was my cousin-the whispers, the judgments, missed birthdays, and holidays. We navigated missed flights, surprise visits, and a long list of reasons against continuing long-distance, like driving on 65's black ice in winter." She released a deep breath and a slight chuckle as if she didn't know whether to laugh or cry. "We took risks with our lives, yet we always managed to find our way back."

Julien's jaw tightened. "Because we wanted to. We chose it every time. We chose each other. Every flight, every fight, every damn time we could've walked away. And now, when we finally got it, marriage, a weekend to breathe. We're here now, when it all breaks?"

Janelle's voice cracked, raw. "I want us to choose it again.

But we can't, can we? We don't have a choice to choose us again. Do we? It gets ripped out from under us. This is so unfair."

Julien pulled her into his chest and held her tighter. The kind of hold that remembered the miles, the silence, the faith it took to get here. He pressed his cheek to her temple and spoke low, steady. "Unfair. Yeah, sure feels that way. Is being loved, being chosen unfair? Is the truth, when it finally rises, unfair, or just the path finally showing us where it was always leading?"

She didn't answer.

Julien steadied himself. "Love doesn't form a straight line; it bends and curves like a river. And sometimes it crashes over rocks, to make us stop and look at who we've become. Babe, maybe that's what this is. Just the bend."

His words settled in her chest like breath after tears when they heard a tap at the door. Janelle rose, her limbs slow with ache, her heart still tethered to his. She opened the screen door. Eva stood there like a question the river had carried to their shore. The last time she stood there, her fists curled with fury. She'd come blazing with the truth no one wanted, not even the brother of the man who once held her through the night. She had tried to say it calmly, to reason. But when Justice didn't answer the way she needed, the fire took over. 'She's gonna marry her damn brother," she'd spit, "and no one's saying nothing. Not Red, not his God, not even you. You gonna let that happen, soldier?" She'd watched his hand clench the door frame, his mouth too tight for honesty. And she'd walked away knowing he wouldn't do what needed doing. Now, she stood at the same door, heat in her throat again, but not from rage. From restraint. From love, wrecked and reclaimed. This time, it wasn't about busting in. It was about being let in. She took a breath and knocked again. Softly.

"I'm sorry to interrupt," she said when Janelle appeared, her voice hoarse and shaking. "But I've got something pounding on my chest like it's trying to crush me." Her hand brushed the frame. "I don't even know if you want to hear the truth, but it's yours, and the piece I owe you." A pause, a breath. "May I come in?"

Janelle hesitated. "Why not?" she murmured, as if it no longer mattered who came bearing what. She was drowning in the truth, too tired to kick to the surface. With a flick of her wrist, she waved Eva in.

Eva stepped inside, stood, and nodded to Julien. Her hands were clasped tightly like they might fly apart otherwise. "I'm sorry you both had to find out like this. Janelle, I left home when I was young. My mom was mad, and my dad was absent. I stayed at Miss Lilly's for a bit and worked for a doctor whose wife had died. Thought I was helping him, but I got pregnant. He helped me end it. I didn't want a kid, and he didn't want to start a new family. He had kids already."

Janelle and Julien exchanged a glance, inching closer together.

"Taking that life, it broke something in me. I started drinking. High-end stuff from his liquor cabinet at first. Then, cheaper, harsher bottles. I kept my job, but I lost myself. Eventually, I quit. Drinking replaced the job. I wanted to change. I wanted to hope. I thought I had found it at Solidarity. That's where I met the Reverend. He prayed with me and tried to help. We got too close. I thought maybe I'd found love."

Looking at Julien, "but your father never said the words. And I knew he wasn't leaving the church lady." She lit a cigarette, hands shaking slightly. "No, he couldn't leave the church lady, and I couldn't stay with a baby in me. So, I left town." She said it plainly, no heat, just history. "Stayed with my cousin Bernie in Yellow Springs, up in that hot attic with the slanted roof and no fan. Told folks I had female troubles. Truth is, I was growin' you, and hiding," her gaze fixed on Janelle.

She flicked an ash into a water glass on the table. "Wore that wool coat like armor, even when it was too hot to breathe. Bernie said I smelled fusty and looked like fear. I told her the coat was the only thing holdin' me together." Her voice cracked. "Went nine months without a drop. Not even a swallow of communion wine. Sang songs at the window so you'd know me by the sound, if not by name. Named you in my prayers, even when I knew I'd have no right."

She took a long drag and blew the smoke away from Janelle. "I found my way back to the porch a few times, trying to get up my nerve to tell Red where he could shove his secret. I hid under that big ass coat. After you were born, I found my courage and came back to Oakwood. Didn't say much. They started callin' me crazy, Crazy Eva. No matter. They didn't know I just gave away my baby and had to keep livin' like I hadn't. Red said you had to be adopted, safe, loved, and cherished. I couldn't fight that." Eva shifted, her voice trembling. "You were part of something sacred, even if the world wouldn't see it that way. I didn't know how. But I never stopped watching. I always showed up, lingered. Always on the porch."

It was as if Janelle stepped out of her grief and into a saga filled with secrets and sorrow, she hadn't known she was part of. She held on to Julien's arm, not just for balance, but to prevent slipping under the weight of Eva's words. Her eyes pierced through Eva's soul, each word drawing a new line, each breath introducing a woman she did not recognize.

She didn't see a crazy woman. She saw a mother. A woman with dignity, and a choice concealed in a dark night. A choice that cost her, a grief born in silence and carried in plain sight. Janelle's heart thundered against her chest, loud and frantic, like a train barreling through a too-narrow tunnel. Then, BOOM. The sound cracked the air wide open, rattling the walls and snatching the breath from her throat.

Julien jumped up. "What was that?"

A shout from outside. "Smoke."

"The barn."

"Fire!" someone screamed from the street.

Olive dashed from the barn's side entrance, coughing, her hair wild and her blouse covered in soot. "It's the hay bales, they exploded!"

Marcus ran in from the street, ahead of the trucks, panting and scanning his surroundings. "It must've been heat buildup and friction. I saw the flash."

Olive looked back, eyes wide with fresh horror. "Caesar!"

Julien grabbed her by the arms. "He's in there?"

"He was in there! He followed me earlier. I didn't see him leave!"

Julien took off at a dead sprint toward the fire. "Caesar!"

Marcus didn't hesitate. "I'll go with you!" he yelled, dashing after him.

Smoke curled into the sky. Sirens wailed closer. Janelle, Olive, and Eva clung to each other in the field, watching the men run into the fire while the barn burned. The fire trucks arrived in a blur of red, accompanied by screaming sirens. Hoses were uncoiled, and water surged toward the blaze, hissing where it met the flames.

Inside the barn, smoke swallowed everything in sight. Julien's voice cracked through it. "Caesar! Caesar!"

Barking. Faint at first, then louder.

"This way!" Marcus shouted, coughing violently as he followed the sound.

They pushed through debris and intense heat, stumbling toward a corner near the tack room. There, hidden behind a pile of scorched feed sacks, was Caesar, curled up, whimpering, his black fur singed around the ears.

"I got him!" Julien cried, scooping the dog into his arms.

"Get out!" Marcus barked. "I'm right behind!"

Julien charged out of the barn with Caesar limp in his arms. Firefighters parted to let him through as water continued to pound the flames. He collapsed onto the ground, cradling the dog. "He's breathing, but barely," Julien gasped.

A firefighter dropped to his knees beside them. "He's in shock, overcome with smoke. Keep him warm."

Olive knelt beside Julien, sobbing into her blouse. "Lord, not my dog. Not my dog, too."

Janelle fell to her knees and laid her hand on Caesar's side. His chest rose and fell shallowly. "Come on, baby. Come on, you stubborn old dog," she whispered.

After the fire was contained, the firefighters began packing up their equipment as the barn continued to smolder. Cradling Caesar, Julien rose to his feet and walked toward the porch. Olive fell into step beside him. "We've got to get him to a vet," she said urgently.

"I'll drive," Julien said. "He's going to make it."

Marcus emerged from the haze, coughing and looking gutted. "I was working on getting those hay bales moved," he muttered. "I just wanted the place to be finished for the wedding."

Julien met his eyes, firm but not angry. "We'll figure that out later. Right now, we need to save this dude."

Janelle and Eva hovered by the porch, hearts racing. Eva's arms wrapped tightly around Janelle like she could shield her from what had just happened, and maybe what was still to come. The char-filled scent lingered in the air as neighbors drifted back to their homes, murmuring prayers and promises of help.

Red and Mildred pulled up slowly, their car crunching over the gravel. They stepped out with solemn expressions. Red held a small bundle of sympathy cards and wrapped dishes from the repast. Mildred was carrying a basket of folded memorial programs. They weren't there for the fire; they hadn't even known. But they had come to check in, to deliver condolences the old-fashioned way. Perhaps to sit for a minute, to bear witness to the grief that hadn't fully unfolded.

Eva drew Janelle in, her arms tightening as she looked at Red and Mildred, her eyes softer than anyone had ever seen. Her voice was steady but low. "Some things have to burn down before they can be rebuilt."

Janelle didn't flinch this time. She rested her head briefly on Eva's shoulder, not in surrender, but in recognition. "Promise me you'll finish the story," she whispered. "One day. I want to hear it, start to finish." Then what she spoke to Eva, shattered the silence between them like stained glass in sunlight. "Your story matters. You matter. And I want to know you, not just what they told."

Eva blinked hard. It wasn't an invitation into the family, not yet. But it was a door cracked open, wide enough to breathe.

And, even in the thick of her own unraveling, Janelle had made room for the broken parts of someone else's story, too. That small reach across the wound was how healing began, not all at once, but in whispers, in presence, in the quiet decision to try.

The porch heard it all.

Not just the words, but the way they landed. The truth, when spoken aloud, didn't just echo. It rearranged. It watched the fire, the frantic run, the rescue, the way hands reached for fur and faith. It saw the old dog carried like a child, and it knew, some things will never be the same.

It listened as Eva stood at the rail, holding both grief and grace. It watched Janelle lean, not to collapse, but to tether herself. And when Eva whispered, "Some things have to burn down before they can be rebuilt."

The porch had seen it before. And as Janelle rested her head against the shoulder of a woman she was just beginning to understand, the porch didn't creak. It didn't groan. It simply held, like always. Because some truths scorch. And some stories are rebuilt from ash.

# NINETEEN

# GUMBO

A COOL BREEZE carried the scent of hickory along the tree-lined driveway, while sunlight slipped through the angel oak and traced patterns on the porch. Days had folded into each other like linens after a long wash. Time hadn't healed these souls yet, but it had taken the sting out of the air and made space for deep breaths and daily things. The family, bruised but still intact, was learning to live with what was lost and lean gently into what remained.

Caesar, triumphant from surviving the fire and the vet visit, sunbathed on the porch. Quiet chatter floated like cotton in the gentle breeze, as Janelle and Julien nestled under the Angle Oak, their voices competing with chirping birds. The Goodman, DuBois, and Boudreaux kinfolk had gathered again, less for ceremony now, more for comfort.

Olive settled on her truck seat while Red and Mildred reclined comfortably on the porch swing in hushed conversation. Eva leaned against the black lacquer card table, swirling the ice-clinking cubes in her glass of Coca-Cola, her cigarette dangling lazily between two fingers. For once, she wasn't guarded or circling–just letting herself be.

Suddenly, a blue jay swooped down, landing boldly in front of the recovering dog. Caesar perked up, his nose twitching in curiosity, before he playfully lunged forward, snatching the delicate bird in his mouth. With a gleeful leap, he trotted towards the edge of the porch, opened his jaws wide, and sent the startled blue jay soaring into the sky.

"Good boy! Who's hungry?" Julien chimed in with a grin. "Mom has a table reserved for us at the restaurant. Who's hungry?"

Almost as if on impulse, the family sprang into action. Olive moved quickly across the gravel to the cottage to grab her handbag. Janelle headed for the Lexus, which was parked in the driveway. Red and Mildred tidied the porch with light-hearted banter, and Eva lingered at the card table, uncertain. Mildred turned to her, warmth softening the corners of her face. With curiosity shining in her eyes, the church-lady asked. "You want to come with?" Her face brightened with a subtle nod of approval. "Why not?"

It was simple. Just enough. Eva blinked, surprised by the invitation- no edge, no qualifier, no hesitation. Mildred gave a slight shrug, like she'd finally let go of something heavy. Eva straightened her back, brushed her palms on her slacks, and stepped forward. She glanced at Janelle, who getting into her car, seeking silent permission. Janelle nodded, and with that, their excursion began.

Olive caught it all. The grace in it. The quiet work of forgiveness that didn't need a pulpit, just a porch and a woman brave enough to mean it. Eager spirits lifted them as they stepped into the world beyond the porch.

At Cayenne's Creole Table, laughter and the clinking of tableware filled the air. The family sat around a large rectangular table by the window, the scent of gumbo, cornbread, and pickled jalapenos weaving around them like a sacred song. Marcus arrived just after the group, flinging open the door with a dramatic flair and proclaiming, "I brought my appetite and an apology, guess which one's heavier?" He gave Caesar a playful scratch on the head. "Glad to see you still stealing the spotlight, old man." The table chuckled, tension dissolving just a little more.

Penny, the town herald, appeared like a torrid wind through the front door, strutting toward their table with her purse swinging at her side. "Hey, look at y'all! Everyone's here," she said, hands on hips. "I guess the wedding is postponed with the barn burning and all..." Olive's eyes narrowed. Julien looked away, jaw tight. Janelle's lip trembled as she turned her face to the horizon and began to cry.

Mildred sat up straighter, her voice crisp. "Well, you go on and take that news back to wherever you got it, missy."

"Yeah, rumor monger," said Eva, rising to her feet slowly. "And when there is some news, we'll tell it."

Penny blinked, mouth slightly open, then offered a nervous chuckle and backed away, waving her hand as she turned. "Okay then, y'all carry on." She strutted out with the same veracity with which she arrived. The family turned back to one another, their bond, though weathered, gathering strength in the warmth of a shared meal. Cayenne appeared from the kitchen with a flourish. "Alright, y'all. First up, gumbo so rich it might just solve your problems. And jambalaya hot enough to make you forget 'em."

Bowls were passed, spoons dipped, and the laughter returned, this time deeper, rounder, and more rooted in the promise of moving forward. Janelle set her spoon down again and looked at the table. The clatter of silverware quieted once more. She found comfort in her thoughts as she stared at the orchid flower arrangements artfully displayed on the glass tops over teak tables. Soft violets and creams from weathered planters blended seamlessly with the restaurant's Creole aesthetic, lush and storied, effortlessly sensual, matching Cayenne's aura like a signature scent that lingered in every corner she passed.

Janelle allowed herself to quietly muse. *The orchids are my favorite*, she smiled faintly, *but I've always been fascinated by the pitcher plant. We have a whole patch near the front porch. They catch insects and small creatures.*

Janelle spoke up, voice steady. "The honeymoon will not be cancelled. Julien and I are still going away… just not as newlyweds. Call it a sibling sabbatical, if that helps." She let the silence settle, then added, with a half-smile that didn't quite reach her eyes. "Besides," Janelle said, a wry tilt to her voice, "this family isn't exactly conventional now, is it?" No one challenged her because they couldn't.

Eyes passed between the elders, Red, Mildred, Olive, and Eva, each of them holding their breath, memories rising like ghosts they couldn't wrangle anymore. But no one said a word. Maybe because they knew their part in the story had ended here. The rest was up to the children, no longer children, now tasked with deciding how to carry the truth forward.

There was a collective breath, a soft exhale around the table. Heads nodded. Julien reached for Janelle's hand beneath the table, and he lowered his gaze. Olive inhaled sharply, Red and Mildred sat like pillars of salt, stilled by the weight of what they could not change, resolving not to confront again.

Even Cayenne paused in mid-stride, her platter of beignets hovering like an offering. Then, with a shrug and smile curved with sass and something softer, she declared, "Well, hell, if I had a bet on a broken bunch to make something whole, I'd put all my chips right here." She winked at Olive, nodded toward Julien and Janelle's clasped hands, and let her gaze settle, almost tenderly, on the tender tangle that was Red, Mildred, and Eva. "I've seen worse turn out beautiful."

Eva had been fighting a nuisance all afternoon, not the

surface kind, but the kind that settles like a pressure sore. It had been several days since her last drink, and today, she pressed hard on all the places still tender.

Her eyes welled up like a rippling pond, the tears rolling down her cheeks. Cayenne reached over and gently rubbed her back. Eva wasn't just sad. She was agitated. Her fingers tapping the rim of her Coke, her eyes scanning the restaurant like a cornered animal. "This jones is pulling me, she muttered, her voice cracking. I'm trying to live right, for the family, for ya'll. But I need…"

Cayenne leaned closer, her hand steady on Eva's spine. "You're doing fine, honey. You're right here with us."

Eva shook her head, eyes glistening. "But I want a drink. I want a damn drink so bad I can taste it. And I know I gotta choose. The family, or the bottle. And Penny flapping her mouth just now…" Her voice faded into a whisper.

The table remained quiet, reverent.

Eva stood abruptly. "I'm sorry. I need to make a quick run." She turned and walked briskly toward the door, her heels clicking, her head held high, and her shoulders trembling. Cayenne looked after her, then back at the table. "Gotta work out your own salvation, as the good book says," she quipped.

Red blinked, caught off guard. He tilted his head, a wry smile curling at the edges of his mouth. "Didn't think you read that part in the good book," he muttered, more amused than judgmental.

Cayenne arched a brow. "I've read plenty, Reverend. Just didn't memorize it in King James."

Olive watched the door swing closed behind Eva. She didn't move. Didn't speak. Not everything needs fixing, she thought. Some things just need holding.

Everyone knew. And just like that, the meal resumed, more tender, more present. Bold love and bone-deep truth, despite everything, had made room at the table—and there would be room enough on the porch when they returned.

# TWENTY

# CHANGING TIDE

Bequia Island, Grenadines

THE SAND ON the island of Bequia was like sifted flour, settling softly under the feet of Janelle and Julien as they made their way down a narrow path framed by wind-tossed palms. The beach, half-hidden from the world, curved gently, like it had been waiting for them to arrive with their wounds and silences.

Janelle carried her sandals in one hand, the other wrapped loosely in Julien's. Her sundress danced around her knees with every breeze. He had barely spoken since they landed, but now his thumb rubbed small circles into her palm. That tender intimacy sufficed for the moment. "I think the world might end quietly," she said suddenly.

Julien blinked, the sound of waves threading between her words. "What makes you say that?"

She looked out at the pale turquoise sea. "Because when the loud part's over, there's always this quiet. And it's in the quiet where things fall apart or back together."

He didn't answer right away. Instead, he bent to scoop a skipping stone, rubbed it between his fingers, and spun it across the break. "We used to be anchored way out where the water is honest. You feel that too, right?" He said, pulling Janelle in close. "Like we knew the current. But now it feels like we are caught in the tide. I want to see where we land when everything settles."

Janelle stepped closer, resting her head gently on his shoulder, feeling the warmth radiating between them. "You with the water metaphors," she said, brushing the windblown hair off her face. "Funny thing, you know I am not a great swimmer, but I feel the current pulling me too. We are not who we were, and our feelings have not caught up with this new reality. At least for me, anyway. When I look at you, I still see the same person. That's something special." A soft chuckle escaped her lips, and Julien smiled, their hearts weaving a quiet connection in the moment's embrace.

In the distance, a fisherman in a small boat sang an old tune, his voice curling across the water like smoke from a cooking fire. Nearby, a stray dog flopped in the shade of a coconut tree and let out a long, satisfied sigh. Somewhere behind them, a vendor laughed over a domino game with two old men. The world, somehow, was still turning.

Julien kissed her forehead, soft and reverent. "Are we ready for what tomorrow brings?"

They slow-walked. No plans. No wedding. No labels. Just them, and the changing tide.

***

Janelle sat on the shaded veranda of their hillside cottage, curled in a wicker chair. A honey-hued hush blanketed the morning, broken only by the rhythmic flutter of palm leaves and the distant putt-putt of a fishing boat. The ocean whispered low and steady, like it held secrets only the island could understand.

She had woken up early, restless from dreams that drifted in and out of memory. The letter had been waiting in the zippered side pocket of her suitcase, just as Olive said it would be. Justice's handwriting on the envelope was instantly recognizable, deliberate, and weighty. The kind of penmanship that felt like it came from a man who built things with his hands. She traced the crease on the envelope with her finger. Then, heart thudding quietly in her chest, she opened it.

***

*Janelle, my sweet daughter,*

*If you're reading this, it means I'm gone, not gone in the ways that*

175

*matter, but not here in the body. There were two letters, one for while I was alive, and one for after I was gone. I gave both to my wife, the one who always knew when to hold tight and when to let go. She was in charge of handing out the right one. Looks like this is the one you get. First thing, you know I was never much for fancy words. But I've always been a man who tried to think his way through storms. I did a lot of thinking during the war.*

*Thought even more when I came home. And most of all, I thought hard when your mama and me brought you home to stay. To tell the truth, I didn't fully know what we were getting into. Your mama did. She prayed for you. When you came, her prayer was answered, so she never questioned it, not once. I did, sometimes, not because I didn't love you, but because I wondered if I'd be enough. Now you're wondering too. I know. What does your life mean now that you've got the truth about how it all started? And baby, I won't lie to you, truth can knock the wind out of you. But the truth also clears the air. You can breathe better once it's out there. We can't change who you came from. But what we could do, what we did do, was decided to love you. Not because we had to. Because we wanted to. Because God whispered your name into our lives, and we said yes. Many moments shaped our time as a family. The day we brought you home, your first steps, the time you stood up to that bully in the third grade, field trips, and shopping trips. I remember them all. What I don't remember is a day I didn't think of you as mine. Now I imagine you might feel like you lost something. Maybe even feel like a piece of your life wasn't real. But hear me. Nothing about the way we loved you was pretend. We just made the best decision we could at the time, and we did it from love. You've got a lot to carry now. But you don't have to carry it all at once. One day at a time. One moment at a time. And if I could ask you for anything, it would be this. Don't let the past take your now. You are, without a doubt, our daughter, no question, no condition, no shame. No matter what, you will always be our girl.*

*Love always,*

*Dad*

"You will always be our girl," her dad's words wrapped around her heart like a hug. She stretched her arms, wiggled her toes, and twirled her hair. The memory returned, fresh like it was yesterday, in third grade, when she stood up to the bully.

You and Mom came to school because some mean girls were making fun of me; they said I was adopted. Their words felt like they had borrowed them from someone else.

Those bullies picked on almost every girl who didn't stand up to them. They told me how things were done and the rules I had to follow. They acted as if I needed their permission to sit with certain friends, decide who to talk to, and who to avoid.

One day, feeling a little brave, I walked up to the bossy girl standing by her cubby with her two sidekicks. I got super close to her, close enough to smell her fruity bubble gum. To make sure she heard me, I spoke with a fierceness, even though my lips were shaking, and my eyes were watery. "You aren't the boss of me! You can't tell me who to talk to, where to go, or who I can eat lunch with. You don't get to make my rules! I'm Janelle Grace Goodman." I poked the ringleader in the chest.

"I'm my daddy's girl, and he says I make the rules. Got it?" Then I poked her again and strolled away.

Now, twirling her hair again, she leaned back on the wicker chair outside the rented cottage. The wind carried the scent of sea salt and hibiscus. She watched the turquoise waves kiss the shoreline, listened to the rhythmic hush of the tide, and let the memory settle in beside her like an old friend.

"Justice Goodman is my father. Olive Goodman is my mother. This shapes my identity and guides my path forward, she whispered." A seagull cawed overhead. The sun warmed her skin. And for the first time in days, she let herself feel light. Julien was napping in the hammock nearby, one hand draped over the edge, his book open across his chest. Tomorrow, they might talk again about what comes next. But today, she had her father's words, the sea, and this moment.

Janelle scooted over on the silky sand to where Julien lay in the hammock. She studied him as if seeing him for the first time, skin the shade of cocoa, six feet of lean physique, sculpted muscles. He maintained his swimmer's shape even after college. She moved closer to feel his breath on her face. "Hey. You riding a wave out there?" she asked softly.

Julien opened his eyes, smiled, and tucked the book between them.

"What's Marcus Aurelius teaching you today?" she teased.

Julien chuckled and glanced at the cover. Meditations. "That we don't control much, but we can control how we show up in the mess of it all."

Janelle nodded, her eyes soft. "Seems like that's all we've been doing lately."

Julien leaned in, brushing his fingers along her jaw. "Babe. I'm so glad we made this trip; I wouldn't trade this moment with you for anything."

"Not even the old normal?"

He shook his head slowly. "No. This, right now, with you, even in the wreckage, feels more honest than anything else."

They stared at each other a beat too long. The book slipped from between them onto the sand. Julien reached out, cradling her face, and then their lips met, quiet and trembling, the heat of their bodies mingling beneath the Caribbean sun. "I want to kiss you—all over," Julien said, his voice throaty with longing. "I want to touch every inch of you, memorize every curve, and remind myself of what we had." His hands meandered slowly, touching to remember. Janelle shivered beneath his fingertips.

"Julien," she whispered, her voice trembling. "This isn't helping, like this. I can't feel different about you like *this*. I want this. I want you." The tension between right and wrong collapsed under the weight of something truer. "Oh, God, please forgive me," she pleaded, not waiting for an answer. And there, on the edge of goodbye, they let their bodies speak what their hearts hadn't yet figured out how to say. And between time and truth, they let go of everything else.

They awoke wrapped in quiet on the following morning. A

rooster crowed in the distance. A faint rustle of palm leaves drifted through the open shutters. They didn't speak of the night before. Instead, they slipped into the rhythm of the day, sharing stories and soft laughter over a breakfast of sliced mango, johnnycakes, and coconut coffee. They toured the island on a borrowed scooter, weaving past goats and schoolchildren, and stopping at a craft market where Janelle bought a hand-woven shawl for her mother and earrings for Eva.

Julien bartered for a book featuring the island's watercolors. He shopped for handmade espadrilles for Cayenne and watercolor notecards for Mildred. He paused at a small stall near the edge of the market, where a striking cream straw boater hat caught his eye.

Janelle glanced up from the display of cufflinks as Julien held up the hat, his voice softer than usual. "Hey, what do you think, for my father? The black and blue band reminds me of something my father once wore, back when he carried himself like a man untouched by time or consequence. I think it suits him, tall, striking, almost islandly in the way he walks into a room like it owes him sunlight."

Janelle studied the brim, then Julien's face. There was something in the way he held it, not just asking for style, but for something more. The band was embroidered with a delicate curling vine, pale green with tiny blossoms the color of coral. The merchant leaned in, voice low, as if sharing a secret. "That's noyau vine. Native to this island. Islanders say it weaves past and present together, and if you wear it, you carry both wherever you go."

Julien's eyes flicked to Janelle, a question unspoken but heavy in the space between them. Maybe this was what a truce looked like, not a surrender, but a note passed quietly between past and present. She nodded. "He'd like it."

Julien turned without a word and walked to the register. He bought the hat.

The couple spent the afternoon snorkeling in crystal-clear waters, racing each other to the reef, surfacing breathless and smiling. It was almost like they had gone back in time to their early days, when all that mattered was their spark and their ability to make each other laugh. That evening, sun-drunk and sea-tired, they collapsed onto the bed without changing out of their beach clothes. Janelle rested her head on Julien's chest, his steady breath anchoring her to sleep.

***

Before dawn, Janelle stirred. Quietly, she slipped from bed and padded across the cool tile floor. The envelope was exposed in the zipper pocket of her suitcase; Justice's letter was now folded neatly inside her journal. She removed her engagement ring, placed it on the watercolor book, and set it on the wooden nightstand. She scribbled a short note, folded it carefully, and put it beside the ring.

*Julien, thank you for being the safest place I've ever known. I'm riding the wave, not to drift away, but to find my own rhythm in the tide. Bequia reminded me what calm feels like. Now I need to learn how to carry that calm back to us.*

*Love you always, J*

She exited the cottage and entered a waiting car to be taken to the ferry as the sun rose over the water, illuminating a golden path across the sea. And this time, she didn't look back.

# TWENTY-ONE

# OLD OAK TABLE

FROM ITS POST on the old Victorian, the porch had watched the months roll by since the fire, the funeral, and the revelations that split the seams of their lives like a sudden summer storm. Grief had eased its tight grip, and though healing came unevenly, the porch could see it in small ways, like sunlight breaking, bit by bit, through a stubborn cloudy sky.

Olive wanted to show her appreciation to the ladies for all their support, and she invited them to lunch. The aroma of chicken and dumpling soup filled the air as bowls were passed around the old oak table. A cucumber salad was chilled nearby in a crystal dish. The conversation ebbed and flowed; light chatter laced with laughter. Olive leaned forward with a question; her eyes turned to Mildred. "How's Red?" she asked.

Mildred replied that he had been doing much better since his talk with Julien at the church on the day of the funeral, and that he seemed grounded and focused.

"How so?"

"Well, I was listening to him speak on Sunday at church. *You know,* in his sermon, he said, 'there is God stuff and church stuff. God stuff can be church stuff, but not all church stuff is God stuff.' He told the congregation that he made an emotional decision to follow God when he was in Korea. He was frightened and didn't know if he would make it out of there alive. So, he started to negotiate with God. He said his emotion caused him to think transactionally, like, 'God, if you do this, then I will do that.' That's when he realized that surrender to God works from the inside out. He admonished the church to practice what it preaches. So Red and me aim to surrender our will to God. We will see what happens regarding the church, our family, and everything going on in our lives. It feels like we are on the same page. His words led me to reflect on my role as his wife and First Lady. I'm not in charge. *You know?* God is." She talked as if truth was being revealed to her as she spoke. "In the beginning, I was trying to school Red in church stuff and make him into a pastor. I saw all the gifts, *you know?*" Her brow wrinkled and she squinted her eyes, straightening her posture in the chair. "Preaching, teaching, leadership–he had many qualities. But what I didn't understand was if he was ready to step into the role of a servant, to care for and guide others into a deeper relationship with the Lord, when he was figuring that out for himself. I looked past the demons that God hadn't fully worked out of him. Well, *you know*, he is a good leader now, but he went through the fire. Guess— I put the cart before the horse, *you know*."

Mildred nodded her head and lifted her shoulders proudly. "But now, he is helping me become a true follower by seeking God's stuff. God's work will survive the fire, and we will continue doing His work to find out where the true value lies. We are going to follow God and see what happens, *you know.*"

"Wow!" Cayenne said, "Good for y'all. Being on the same page makes all the difference. Red and I? Well, *you know...* history, we tried once, after he came home from the war. He was a different man. But he needed someone like you, Milly, quiet and saved, and I was neither. Yeah, he got the right one, for sure. I'm happy for y'all."

Milly's smile held, but her eyes blinked slower than usual, the way they did when something stung but didn't draw blood. Cayenne kept talking, unaware or unwilling to stop. She was never one to read the room when she had the floor, not out of ignorance, but out of indifference. Cayenne is Cayenne, always has been, and no one at that table felt bold enough to tell her otherwise.

"Yeah, we loved in the wrong season. Still made a beautiful boy, though. I pray that he continues to make amends with Julien. Our son was shook after learning the truth about him and Janelle. I've been tryin' to help Julien understand that what happened to him wasn't only caused by someone else. Like, he contributed big time to the situation, *okay?* It is a hard truth, but he and Janelle have rebelled since college, since they tasted a little freedom. First, knowing, or believing they were cousins, they ignored our advice and entered into a romantic relationship. They were all in when the truth came out."

Olive leaned back and sighed. "I thought it would wear off. Puppy love, *you know?* But those kids went deeper. They trusted each other so much that it was like neither of them wanted to step outside of that comfort zone. Once they hooked up, it was like no one else mattered. I saw it forming and didn't know how to stop it. And I get why some adoptive parents are a little timid when it comes to correcting their kids. They're scared they'll lose their child or hurt them, and they won't recover. Or worse, that they will be rejected. Janelle had her suspicions, and I didn't want her to look deeper than she needed to. I don't know, I thought it would blow over."

She looked down at her hands before continuing, "Well, it came out when it was supposed to come out. Janelle accepted it better after her daddy passed. She read the letter he left her when she was in Bequia. She said it was comforting. I know it would've crushed him if she had come at Justice like Julien did at Red. She lashed out at me instead. And I know it was from pain. I hated to have contributed to that, but honestly, to get through it, I took it like I did all her other outbursts, when I said no to make-up, or when she couldn't go to a party without chaperones. All the mother-daughter storms we've weathered through the years."

"Well, this was more serious than wearing make-up, girl!" Cayenne snapped.

Olive shrugged. "What do you know? You raised a boy."

Cayenne didn't flinch. She gave Olive that look, the one she'd been giving since they were very young, and she started swinging before thinking. "I *did*, by myself," Cayenne said. "Raising a boy doesn't spare us from heartbreak. We had our issues. But that is a story for another day." She reached for Olive's hand, didn't press, just let it be there.

Eva walked up the path looking refreshed and invigorated. She was makeup-free, with silver hair tossed in a bun, bright nail polish, capris, and a white T-shirt. She tapped lightly on the screen door. "Hey, y'all got room for one more? Sorry, I'm late. I just got out of my meeting."

Olive said, "Yes, ma'am. Come in, come in!"

Mildred looked at her and commented, "Eva, you look pretty." She scooted to make room for her seat around the table.

Eva sat down in the chair. "Thank you, I feel good. The 12-step program is helping me, and I have been attending church. It feels good not to be so hard on myself. I am making amends with my broken self and grateful that there is at least something left to repair. *You know,* taking this drinking thing one day at a time. I can't just give up drinking and clap my hands and say that's it, but I surrender it every day I wake up."

She turned to face Mildred. "Mildred, I'm glad you're here. I've been wanting to ask you for your forgiveness. I never asked for your forgiveness. I cheated with your husband, and I was drunk, but I knew I put him in a bad position. We were both in pain; that wasn't passion, it was pain. I'm sorry." Eva was resolute, her voice calm but unwavering. There was no tremble, no shrinking.

Olive sensed that Eva didn't come to beg or unravel; she came to be whole, and the apology wasn't dragged out by guilt; it was offered by a woman who had done her reckoning and come through on the other side.

Mildred reached forward with her hand and accepted her apology. "Eva, I forgave you a long time ago. I found my peace and hoped you would see that forgiveness has always been open to you; you only needed to reach out for it."

Olive piped up, "Well, look at God! Miss Lilly was right. When light steps into darkness, the darkness is overcome by the light."

Eva asked, "How is Janelle?"

Olive said, "She's good, throwing herself into her work."

"Good, good," Eva smiled.

Then Olive leaned forward a bit and sipped her tea. "I wanted to get your opinions on something. The board wants me to consider becoming the community manager of the HOA for the newly designated Oakwood Historical District. I've been thinking about it."

Cayenne raised an eyebrow. "The Historical District? With all of them busybodies and their yard flags and driveway drama? Are you sure you want that kind of extra stress?"

"I'd hire help around the property," Olive replied with a shrug. "Someone to help with the upkeep, errands, and whatnot. I won't be out here trimming hedges with a clipboard in my hand."

Cayenne chuckled. "Well, you can start by doing something about Bette Day and that double-wide! Either make her pave over the gravel or plant some flowers and put a fresh coat of paint on that monstrous thing for goodness' sake. That woman's yard got more moods than a teenager with no Wi-Fi! Oh! That reminds me. Who's cooking for her now? Olive, if you're going to be doing that HOA business, we'd better come up with a plan to feed that woman. Wouldn't want her burning down the place. Justice would haunt me if I didn't help her some kinda way."

They all laughed, the kind that shook their shoulders and lifted the weight of months past. The sun crawled through the trees, and it felt like spring again for the first time in a while.

Around Olive's table, grace was served as generously as dumpling soup. This wasn't just a meal–it was mending. The porch, like Olive herself, had held secrets, heartache, and heat, but now it held something softer, renewal.

# TWENTY-TWO

# NEW DAY, NEW LIFE

THE WARM FAMILIARITY of city rhythm had swallowed Janelle whole since she returned to Chicago, and she let it. She had thrown herself back into work with the kind of precision and zeal only heartbreak and clarity could summon. The office felt familiar again, yet different, as if something had been stripped away and rebuilt.

She arrived that morning dressed in a charcoal-gray Armani suit, with a cream silk blouse tucked sharply at the waist, her hair pulled into a sleek ponytail. She stepped out of the elevator in time with Nina Simone's *Feeling Good* playing on the Muzak.

Her heels clicked in tempo with the rhythm as she moved through the glass doors into the firm's open floor plan. Her team was already gathered. Stanley gave a slight nod. Candace, the online community manager, sat with a laptop open and raised a brow. Janelle stood at the head of the table, poised and confident. "Alright, team," she began, a smile on her face. "Let's give Stanley a round of applause for handling media for Cordel Zane while I was away. His hard work and dedication have truly made a difference!" Cheers and applause erupted in the room, celebrating Stanley's efforts and leadership.

"Let's get to work, shall we?" Janelle continued. "Zane is already pulling heat. The media is circling, and we're going to give them a reason to stay. We need a brand story, narrative arcs, a few controlled leaks, and a short film campaign." She glanced at Stanley. "You and I will draft the public persona angle. Candace, prep social platforms. Content needs to feel like it was made in his mother's kitchen. Authentic, heart, grit. We need to humanize the muscle." The room buzzed with energy. Janelle took her seat and smiled to herself. It felt good to lead again.

Later that afternoon, Janelle was called into the senior partner's office. "Janelle," Deborah King motioned for her to sit at the small conference table, facing a glass with stunning views overlooking Michigan Avenue.

"Thank you, Deborah," Janelle answered politely.

"When I first founded Zenith, it was just me and one high-profile client, anxiously awaiting a major contract signing that felt like a dream. Navigating his career opened the door to two more clients, top picks, and elite athletes who believed in our vision. Fast forward ten years, and here we are, proudly establishing ourselves as one of the top sports management agencies in Chicago. This journey couldn't have been possible without your invaluable leadership. You've been doing impressive work," she said, sliding a leather-bound folder across the desk with a hint of nostalgia in her voice. "I want to offer you the opportunity to transition into agent representation, endorsements, and PR. You've got the instincts we need. I'd like for you to consider my proposal."

Janelle opened the folder slowly, eyes widening. It wasn't just a promotion. It was a path. After everything, after the secret that shattered her foundation, after breaking off an engagement to the only man she ever pictured beside her, after wondering if her entire life had been a well-told lie, this was something that made sense. Something earned. Something she could hold.

This opportunity didn't just validate her talent; it reminded her who she was before the storm. Before the porch talks and DNA truth-telling, before she witnessed her mother's eyes go glassy with grief. It said she was still here. Still capable. Still becoming. It was more than a title. It was a mirror, held up just in time. She would not doubt herself this time. She accepted the offer without hesitation.

That night, she dined with Fern, who was visiting for the weekend, and Stanley at a rooftop bistro overlooking the river. The sky burned a pink and gold hue, casting a warm glow over the Chicago skyline. They laughed over cocktails, and their voices competed with soft jazz playing in the background. Janelle, in a celebratory mood, giddily chose mini crab cakes and truffle Parmesan fries from the menu. The friends savored each bite while exchanging stories from their lives. They toasted to her new chapter; a sentiment filled with hope and excitement for the future.

"You always had the fire," Stanley said, his eyes reflecting admiration.

"You never stopped believing," Janelle replied, her smile wide as she felt the support of her friends surrounding her, filling her with gratitude and determination to embrace the adventures ahead.

*** 

The next morning, sunlight spilled across Janelle's hardwood floors like melted honey. The skyline blinked through her windows, still waking. Fern was curled up on the couch in one of Janelle's oversized hoodies, her legs tucked under her and a satin bonnet slightly askew. She relaxed as she often had in Janelle's studio during their college days. She looked like she belonged there. Janelle emerged from the kitchen with two steaming espresso cups. "Hope you still like it bold," she said, handing Fern her mug.

"Like my men," Fern smirked, taking a sip. "So, what's next for you, J?"

Janelle inhaled deeply. "I've made a decision."

Fern paused mid-sip, her eyes narrowing playfully. "This sounds like one of those Oprah-worthy revelations. Do tell."

"I'm applying to law school," Janelle said. Her voice didn't tremble. "I want to become a full-fledged sports agent. Not just PR, not just endorsements. The whole damn deal."

Fern blinked. "You tryna run PR and law school? Girl, you better be sleeping inside a law book with a nap timer taped to your forehead."

Janelle laughed, soft but steady. "I'm ready, Fern. It's time. I need a new beginning."

Fern raised an eyebrow and glanced around the room. "New beginning, huh? Not by the looks of it. Julien still got prime real estate on that mantel. It's like the *museum of us* up there."

Janelle turned her eyes to the collection of framed memories: their first college game, a goofy New Year's party, and their trip to the Bahamas. "Julien was-*is*-my best friend," she said. "Even if we can't be together. That part… That part I want to keep. He knows me."

"Well," Fern said, curling her legs tighter, "you sure got a funny way of showing it. Y'all haven't spoken in how many months now?"

Janelle sighed. "We will when we're ready. There's still healing to do, and the distance is still too close. I need to find peace with what is, not with what could have been. And I need a distraction, law school, this next move. No more middle woman. I want a seat at the table."

Fern scoffed. "Girl, if you didn't build the table, you designed the blueprints, chose the wood, and passed out the place cards. You just forgot to sit yourself down."

Janelle smiled, warmth rising in her cheeks. "Alright then," she said, lifting her mug. "Let's toast to that!"

Fern raised hers in return. "To the future Counselor Goodman. And not sleeping."

Janelle grinned. "C'mon, let's get dressed. We're going out. I need sushi, mimosas, and compliments."

Fern was already on her feet. "I'm putting on lashes for this."

***

Janelle and Fern stepped out for lunch at a chic restaurant in a high-rise near The Loop. Sunlight lit the room, quiet conversations flowed, and plates clinked between sips of iced tea and bites of sandwiches. A tall man walked up with a surprised smile. "Fern?"

They both looked up.

Fern squinted, then broke into a grin. "Grunt? I mean *Francis?*"

He laughed. "Been a long time."

"What are you doing here?" she asked, eyes scanning him.

I'm an assistant football coach at DePaul. Fern's gaze dropped to his left hand, noting the absence of a ring. "Damn. Guess I'm going to have to move to Chicago."

Francis raised a brow. "Where are you living now?"

"Vegas. Real estate. It's working for me."

"Really? I got a place out there," he said, grinning. "Stay there part-time."

"You looking to sell?"

"Maybe not," he said, eyes still locked on her.

They laughed and exchanged numbers, and the energy at the table shifted, light and flirtatious, with something new unfolding just beneath the surface.

# TWENTY-THREE

# SIBLING HITS DIFFERENT

Chicago, Illinois

Autumn, 2004

THE HOTEL LOBBY shimmered under the soft glow of chandeliers. Janelle stepped off the elevator onto the marble floors wearing a tailored cream pantsuit, heels clicking confidently, her tote slung effortlessly over her shoulder.

The gala reception was already humming inside the ballroom, and her name was printed on the evening's program as a featured panelist. She was halfway to the speaker's reception area when she heard him, velvety, unmistakable, threaded with memory.

"Janelle?"

Her body responded before her mind could catch up, like it always had with him. A tilt of the head, a pull in her chest, the brief flutter of something half-remembered. But then her thoughts caught up, sharp and sober, reminding her that love now required new terms. She straightened, reset her breath, and turned.

Julien stood just beyond the spiral column near the hotel lounge, hands in his pockets, framed like a still from a film, half shadow, half-light, the slightest smile ghosting his face as if he'd been waiting for this scene to unfold all along.

Walking in his direction, she asked, "What are you doing here?" blinking as if the hotel itself had conjured him from memory.

"General Contractors Electrical Engineering Conference. Staying here all week," he said. "What about you?"

"Networking gala. Women in Media and Sports. I will be speaking on brand integrity."

They both smiled. It wasn't awkward, not yet. Familiarity softened the tension. But it still tugged at their corners.

"Can we talk for a minute?" Julien asked, motioning toward the mezzanine.

"Of course," Janelle moved closer.

They stepped into the quieter space above the lobby, overlooking the city through sweeping glass windows. "You look good," he said gently.

"Thanks. As do you."

They maintained a cautious space between them.

"I'm glad to see you," he said. "Been meaning to reach out."

"Same. I just… I didn't know how to."

Julien nodded. "I started therapy. It's helping me unpack some things, not just about us, but about my parents, my identity, and seeing you not as mine but as my sister."

Janelle looked away, out at the skyline. "I'm proud of you. I'm sure that is not easy. You're brave."

"No, you were always the brave one," he said. "I was the one who clung."

"You loved hard. Honestly. We both did."

He looked at her then, really taking in her appearance. "So why didn't you say goodbye? That morning on the Island."

Janelle swallowed hard. "I did. I left a note." She paused, her voice tightening. "If I'd said those words out loud, if I'd looked you in the eye, I wouldn't have gone. And I had to go. I had to protect what I had left. If I stayed, I would've lost that too."

They stood quietly.

Julien spoke up. "I don't regret loving you. But I can't keep standing in the same space and pretending it doesn't burn."

Janelle reached out, her fingers brushing his hand, a quiet thanks for the air that shifted between them. "I need to get in there," nodding toward the closing doors. "We'll talk soon? Not to fix anything, just to keep going."

Julien brushed his palm over her fingers. "Sis, huh?"

She smiled. "Bro?"

Julien pulled her into a long, quiet hug.

Then they parted, again. But this time, with maturity, and maybe, finally, a little peace.

# TWENTY-FOUR

# DEEDS

EVA MOSEYED UP to the porch like she did most afternoons, now, her presence becoming a familiar rhythm in Olive's world. But today, something felt off. Olive wasn't in her usual spot on the truck seat, and Caesar was not on guard duty. The sun was at high beam. Both the D100 and the Buick were in the driveway. Eva trusted her instincts and crossed over the gravel walk to the cottage.

Before she heard anything, she smelled something that had burned, not a fire, but the sharp, scorched scent of a forgotten pot. Ray Charles's music played softly in the background. She knocked a few times. After a moment, Olive answered, her silver hair a bit tousled, her expression weary.

"Hey, Olive. Just stopped by to say hi."

"Come on in," Olive said. "I was just going through some papers."

Inside, Eva blinked. The typically tidy space was in disarray. The oak table was strewn with papers, envelopes, half-open files, and a few pieces of unopened mail. Olive appeared disoriented, searching for something that wasn't where it was supposed to be.

"What you looking for, honey?"

"I can't seem to find the deeds to our property. I might want to get shed of some of this land. Justice decided years ago to break up the 60-acre farm into smaller plots. He said not everyone could afford big tracts, but folks deserved a chance to stay in the community, to build and own something of their own. He sold off a good bit to the dairy folks and folks who grew up 'round here. Helped keep them from getting priced out or pushed out. Nine acres is still more'n I need."

Eva glanced around, her eyes scanning the chaos. "You got HOA reports in here with recipe cards. What happened to your file bins?"

"I must've pulled them all out."

Eva moved toward the counter, sifting through a pile of manila folders. She spotted a large envelope labeled *DEEDS* in Olive's neat script.

"Here they are, right here. Is this what you're looking for?"

Olive blinked. "Oh, yes. Lord, Jesus. Right there? Uhm. I

forgot I put them there."

Eva didn't say anything at first while she stepped to the stove. She opened the pot on the stove, wincing at the scorched green beans and potatoes. "Whew, baby. You done smoked these veggies. Maybe we can skim some off the top. Let me help you." She grabbed a spoon and scooped out what she could while Olive moved around slowly, as if trying to retrace her steps.

"You okay, sweetie?" Eva asked gently.

"Oh yeah, I am good," she said, sounding more like she was trying to convince herself. "The HOA, the land, the trust Justice left, it's all stacked up. I keep telling myself I'll get to it, then the days melt together."

Eva nodded slowly. She noticed Olive had her house shoes on the wrong feet. Something in her heart fluttered with worry, but she stayed steady. "Well, how 'bout I help you file some of this away, and we get these beans to behave? Then maybe sit out on the porch for a spell."

"That would be nice. Real nice," Olive said. "It's like a museum over there, though. Sometimes when I'm sitting by myself, I feel like a relic, just me and the ghosts. Most days, the only visitors I receive are folks stopping by to ask how high the hedges should be, when will I address the situation with the woman in the double-wide, or to complain about their neighbor who won't clean up the dog poop, or the pigeon droppings from the adjacent property." She sighed. "Janelle should be visiting soon. She's busy now with law school, you know.

Doesn't pop over on weekends like she used to."

Eva leaned on the counter. "I'm sure she and Julien are keeping their distance for a reason. Secrets made us all sick. But time heals all wounds. I've talked to her a few times. It's getting easier to be open. I'm moving past the shame, and I think she is moving on, too. I'm so thankful to be a branch on this beautiful family tree! Honestly, it's a relief not to have to search for my place among the leaves; there's no pressure to change my position or fit where I haven't been in the past. I truly appreciate where we are and where we are headed!" She nodded slowly, her eyes softening. "Let me help you tidy up some of these papers, give the temp outside a chance to cool. Maybe we can figure out how to bring that porch back to life. It used to be the heartbeat of this place, with lemonade, laughter, and folks dropping by to pass the time. I miss that."

"I'll make us some lunch," Olive offered, turning toward the kitchen.

She walked in, but paused, standing still, her hand resting on the fridge like she'd forgotten why she came in. Eva watched quietly for a second, then spoke up.

"Olive, why don't you sit and relax? You're always doing for everybody else. Let me get you lunch this time. I'll pour myself some tea while I'm at it."

Olive hesitated, then slightly nodded and moved back to the table.

"I'll just have tea, I want the sweet, cold, please," she said softly.

Eva gave her a wink. "Coming up."

A knock came at the screen door.

"Anybody home?" came Marcus's voice.

Olive stood, startled momentarily, then called out, "Marcus? Yes, please, come inside."

He stepped inside, holding the door for a shy young boy who peeked around.

"This is Isaiah, my son," Marcus said.

Eva's eyebrows shot up. "You've been holding out on us, Marcus Cook!"

Marcus laughed sheepishly. "Didn't mean to. He's nine. Stays with me every other weekend. His mom's a principal over in Centerville. Thought I'd bring him by while I check on Miss Olive."

Olive gave Isaiah a soft smile. "Hey there, young man."

Before anyone else could speak, Caesar wandered in from the back porch and trotted straight toward Isaiah. The boy lit up.

"Dad, a dog!" Isaiah exclaimed, dropping to one knee.

He reached out and gently petted Caesar. At first, the old dog gave a little grunt of protest, a one-person canine who never gave his loyalty easily. But after a few seconds, his tail gave a soft thump, stopped, and thumped again.

Marcus and Olive both watched with interest.

"He's getting on real snobby lately," Olive murmured.

Marcus took a breath. "I've been meaning to ask. I was wondering if you might consider renting out Justice's place. I could help around the property. I feel like I could be more useful to you if I were nearby, and Isaiah will be entering middle school and changing schools. His mother agreed to let him attend school in this area, which means I could see him more frequently during the school year, not just in the summer. No pressure, think about it. I hate to see old Victoria shut up like that."

Caesar gave another tail thump as if seconding the motion.

Eva leaned toward Olive. "Well, looks like the committee's already voting."

Olive's gaze lingered on Caesar and the boy beside him. "Perhaps, just perhaps."

As dusk fell, they strolled across the gravel walk to the porch, where it stood silent, sturdy, a watchful guardian with time. It cradled secrets, braved storms, and bore witness to truths unfolding, taking root once more. And now, at last, it could embrace a semblance of peace. For what remained was not merely memory, nor just survival. What lingered was the truth, spoken, shared, and lived. And that was enough.

# TWENTY–FIVE

# CARRY ON

"A RED DOOR? Are you sure about this?" Olive looked at Marcus sheepishly.

"Yes, trust me, Mama Olive, you'll love it. And when we get your window flower boxes up, and you do your magic planting and a little landscaping, this cottage will be ready for Dayton Home & Garden magazine."

Olive shook her head, a little smile breaking through. "Who would have thought?"

A high-pitched voice came from the rear of the house. "Granny Olive! Granny Olive! Look, look what I taught Caesar to do!" Isaiah came bounding around the side yard, excitement bouncing in every step. Caesar followed with the slow dignity of an aging dog trying to keep up with young legs. "Caesar, open the door! Caesar, open the door!" Isaiah called out.

To everyone's surprise, Caesar trotted over and pawed at the screen door's latch until it popped open.

"He can turn on the light, too! And he can open cabinets! When we're not around, you'll always have help, Granny Olive."

Olive laughed. "Can Caesar cook now, too?"

Marcus piped up. "No, but whenever you don't feel like it, we've got you covered."

A black Lexus pulled into the driveway. The sun reflected off the windshield, and when the door opened, Janelle stepped out, her weekender bag in hand, oversized sunglasses perched confidently on her face. She took one look at the remodeled exterior and blinked. "Am I at the correct address?" she asked with a grin. "This place is beautiful, almost idyllic. I love what's going on here. Wow, what a nice job on Mom's house and the Victorian, is that all you, Marcus? Looks amazing!"

Isaiah stepped forward and extended a hand with earnestness. "Hello, I'm Isaiah."

Janelle shook it warmly. "I'm Janelle. I see you got a friend."

"Yes! Want to see what I taught him to do for Granny Olive?" Isaiah said, already turning toward Caesar.

"Isaiah," Marcus interjected gently, "let Miss Janelle get settled first."

Marcus stepped forward. "Can I get your bags, Janelle?"

She handed over the weekender and the keys to the trunk for the rest of her luggage. "Mom is fond of you," Janelle said, nodding toward the house.

"The feeling is mutual," Marcus replied. "I like the balance. Isaiah's mom lives in Centerville, so he gets that sweet, ladylike care when he visits Olive. It's good for all of us."

Janelle raised an eyebrow playfully. "You're not so bad at the sweet part yourself, Mr. Marcus Cook."

He chuckled. "Let's get you inside. Your mom and I have a block party planning meeting to get to."

Janelle paused before following. She looked back at Caesar, who had positioned himself next to Isaiah, his tail thumping slowly and steadily. She joked that that old dog still had a lot of life left in him. He must be on his second or third time around.

From inside, Olive called out, "Y'all coming or what? There's iced tea and blueberry cobbler with your name on it!"

They let the door close behind them, and the porch kept listening.

***

Janelle showered and changed into a comfortable jumper. She tied her hair into a topknot, slipped on her flip-flops, and skipped to her car. She had an important visit to make before the day unfolded.

At the florist on Far Hill, she selected a bouquet of hydrangeas, butterfly gladioli, white orchids, lemon leaf, and sword fern, each bloom a fragment of memory, love, and longing. Carrying the bouquet close to her chest, she returned to the car and made her way to the Dayton National Cemetery.

The plot map led her straight to where Justice was laid to rest. She found his headstone, among the others, dignified and still. She knelt and placed the bouquet gently on the ground, smoothing the grass with her hand. Her eyes locked on the engraving, ...*a good and decent human being, gone but not forgotten.* Leaning close to the earth, she whispered. "Hey, Dad. Life without you has been a journey I never thought much about, but I get it now."

She paused, her throat tight. "You're still my hero. My first love. My anchor. Your letter touched me, and it's been holding me together on days I didn't think I could. I hear your resolute voice in it." She brushed a tear from her cheek. "We had our rough patches, but we loved through them. And right now, I'm learning to let go of not marrying Julien. That's the hardest part. But we're getting there. Together. In our way."

She smiled faintly. "Mom's doing good. She's got help now, Marcus and Isaiah. Her memory slips sometimes, but she's not alone. Caesar's taken a liking to Isaiah. It's funny, like that boy woke something up in him." She looked up toward the sky. "Uncle Red and Mildred, well, you wouldn't believe it, but they're reevaluating things. They may step away from leadership at their church. You'd be proud."

"And Eva, Dad, she's sober. Can you believe it? She's really trying, and I think you're responsible in many ways. I hope you're watching. As for me," her voice cracked again, "I'm in law school. I'm chasing something big. I'm going to be a sports agent, yeah, me. I'm doing it. And every time I think I can't, I hear you saying I can."

"There's a block party tomorrow, Oakwood Community on Liberty Lane. Marcus and Mom are running the show. He's a tenant now, in the Victorian. Did all this work himself, made it shine again. Even the porch, oh Dad, the porch, sturdy as ever, rocking chairs and all. Visitors have slowed since you left, but I think that's about to change."

She lingered for a bit, fingering the earth, remembering his smell, or a hug. She laughed, "God, you're too funny," as a beetle landed on her and tickled her arm. She stood and placed a kiss against her fingertips, then pressed them gently to the headstone. "I love you, Dad. See you next time."

***

When Janelle returned to Liberty Lane, she found the area active with preparations. Barriers had been installed at each end of the street, and volunteers were arranging string lights between poles set in weighted planters. A small crew was assembling a stage near the main entrance, and neighbors bustled about setting up tables draped in gingham cloth, folding chairs in mismatched rows, and brightly colored tents with homemade banners flapping in the breeze.

Right before One Liberty Lane, a banner hung that took her

breath away. It featured her father, Justice Goodman, standing proud in front of the yellow D100 with the Goodman Homes logo floating behind him. And there, just beside him, Caesar, tongue out, tail frozen mid-wag. But what undid her was the watermark behind them, a faint image of herself as a little girl, no more than six, running barefoot toward the barn, her hair flying behind her.

She stopped in her tracks. Tears welled in her eyes before she could blink them away. Overcome, she made her way up the porch steps and settled onto the new swing. It creaked in welcome under her weight. She leaned into the backrest, wrapped her arms around herself, and closed her eyes. She heard footsteps, feeling his presence before she saw his face. A warmth, a pull, just like always.

"Janelle."

She opened her eyes but kept her head down. "Who's asking?"

"That depends," came the reply, low, steady, intentional. "I'm an old friend."

She smirked, not looking at him yet. "An old friend, huh? How do you know me?"

"Well, I know you used to live here until you moved to Chicago. When we were kids, we played tag out by the barn. I know you prefer going barefoot over wearing shoes, like now. Where are your shoes, by the way?"

She cracked a smile.

"I know you like hard candy over chocolate, make mean brownies, and prefer espresso over brewed coffee, and you twirl your hair when you're nervous."

She finally turned to face him. "Oh, you kinda sound like my daddy, but you ain't him. I just left him over there on Gettysburg and Liscum."

Julien chuckled. "That's my J. Still crazy."

"Julien," she whispered. "How are you?"

"I'm good. And you?"

"At peace," she said. "I miss you, though."

"Miss you too." He took a step closer. "I thought I'd stop by today to test my emotions. Seeing you again, it's been a long time. I didn't trust myself to be around you before."

"What we have had," Janelle said, "just doesn't disappear. That would make it nothing. We had something. Now, we must channel it into something wholesome and keep the good. I hope we'll be friends for a long time."

He nodded. "Friends? Okay. Brother is good too."

She grinned. "Okay. Sister. That means we had a connection long before the physical bond."

They hugged tightly for a long time. And for the first time in a while, it didn't ache; it calmed like the mists from an eddy in the Great Miami. Janelle broke the moment with humor. "Sister means I can approve of any new girlfriends." She leaned into a laugh, and Liberty Lane hummed behind them, preparing for a celebration of old roots and new beginnings.

# TWENTY-SIX

# OAKWOOD BLOCK PARTY

June 18, 2005

THE BLOCK PARTY was coming to life. Janelle greeted a few neighbors, sipped on sweet tea, and took in the energy around her. But her breath caught when she spotted Julien across the crowd. He was laughing easily and comfortably, conversing with a striking woman in a fitted pink sundress.

They stood near the lemonade stand, just beneath Justice Goodman's banner. Janelle couldn't hear their exchange but saw the woman gently touch Julien's forearm. Something in the gesture was familiar and natural, and Janelle's gaze lingered.

Marcus appeared at her side, handing her a fire-roasted ear of corn. "That's Jacqueline Hutchins, Principal at Dunbar High School, in Centerville," he whispered, "who happens to be Isaiah's mom."

Janelle nodded slowly. "Ah. Wait, for real? You two have history, and now Julien… you can't make this stuff up!"

"She's beautiful. And a good lady," Marcus said, the admiration plain in his voice. "We had a little thing going on right after I got out of jail. I met her when I was in a re-entry program she facilitated through the chamber. We weren't aiming for forever, just a little company, a little kindness. She'd already weathered a divorce and wasn't looking to fall again. No expectations. But then, boom, Isaiah was on the way. She handled it gracefully, didn't run from it, and never made me feel small for what I hadn't figured out. I respect that. Isaiah changed my whole life. Now I want to be the kind of father he can be proud of. Close, like you and Justice. That kind of love? That kind of steady? I want my son to feel that too."

"She looks kind," Janelle replied. She wasn't sure what she felt, surprised and nostalgic, maybe a twinge of sadness, but no jealousy, not today. Janelle arched an eyebrow. "Well, a principal, huh? Seems more like the president of the Lonely and Broken Men's Club. Y'all show up, and she hands out membership cards and healing."

"She has been seeing Julien for several months. They met in Centerville. He landed a big electrical contract with the district," Marcus said, responding to Janelle's obvious curiosity.

Marcus let the comment hang, then shrugged with a knowing grin. "Hey, don't judge, I was trying to get my mind right. She just happened to be standing there with a map and a flashlight. She left me with a compass, too. His name is Isaiah."

Julien looked up then, across the sea of people, and locked eyes with Janelle. He raised his glass slightly, like old friends do when they see someone still holding a piece of their heart.

Janelle raised hers in return and smiled. Whatever was meant to be next could wait until after the music and the memory-making. A beat dropped from the DJ's booth at the corner of the block. The *Cha Cha Slide* opening bars filled the air, and like clockwork, a wave of cheers rippled through the crowd.

"Oh no," Marcus said, grinning. "We doing this?"

"Looks like we don't have a choice," Janelle laughed.

A few feet away, Julien grabbed Jacqueline's hand, and Marcus corralled Isaiah with a playful nudge as Janelle stepped into the growing line. Left foot stomp, right foot stomp, slide to the left… Caesar barked once and circled the edge of the crowd like an amused chaperone. For one electric moment, the whole block moved as one. Today was about community, family, and truth.

***

Later in the afternoon, Olive sat with Isaiah on the swing. "Granny Olive, did you always live here?" he asked.

She smiled, eyes glinting with sunlight and memory. "Child,

217

I didn't just live here, I grew roots so deep they held other folks up when their storms came." She told him a story about Justice saving a neighbor's double-wide after a fire started while she was cooking, something even Janelle couldn't hear enough. Marcus and Janelle watched from a distance, surprised and moved by Olive's clarity.

Olive began to hum a soft, sweet tune. Isaiah leaned his head against her shoulder. "What you hummin,' Granny Olive?"

"Something my husband, Justice, used to sing when he thought no one was listening."

# TWENTY-SEVEN

# PORCH BUSINESS

LIBERTY LANE HAD quieted once again. The echoes of laughter, clinking dishes, and old-school jams still hovered like perfume in the air, but now only the occasional scrape of folding chairs and hum of stage breakdown interrupted the evening stillness.

The porch was full, just as it had been. Olive sat in a custom-upholstered rocking chair, her shawl, Janelle's gift from Bequia, draped over her shoulders. Red and Mildred had just returned from a pastor's convention and were catching up with Cayenne and Eva about the success of the block party.

"That boy who moved in at the end of the street, Penny's

grandson, he's looking to open a coffee cart," Cayenne said. "Said Oakwood felt at home the minute he set foot here. Reminds me of the early days of Altadena, when I was out in Cali. That's where I got the inspiration to open Cayenne's Creole Table. That place is sacred to many people, built from sweat and second chances. When I told him about my stay out there, Justice always said he wanted Oakwood to feel the same way. A place where folks could grow something real, without worry, only for some developer to come along and pave over their dreams."

Olive nodded slowly, sipping tea. "Younger folks movin' in might just breathe new life into this place."

Marcus and Isaiah returned from a post-party look around, still talking about the neighborhood three-on-three tournament. "You saw that crossover?" Isaiah asked. "I had him slippin',' Daddy!"

Marcus chuckled, "You got lucky. But I won't tell nobody you almost double-dribbled."

Isaiah spotted his mother. "Hey, there's Mom!" he said to his dad.

Julien and Jacqueline approached from the sidewalk, hand in hand. Jacqueline smiled as they neared the porch. She lightly fingered her handbag, searching for the car keys. A few steps ahead, they greeted Marcus and Isaiah.

Marcus nodded to Julien and then, turning to Jacqueline, said, "I'll bring Isaiah home tomorrow if it's okay. He wants to stay and help with the clean-up." Jacqueline gave a permissive nod.

Julien paused for introductions, and when he reached Janelle, he said, "Janelle," nodding toward her as she sat nestled between Cayenne and Eva, sipping from a plastic cup.

Janelle looked up.

"This is Jacqueline," Julien said, motioning gently. "Jacqueline, this is Janelle."

"I've heard so much about you," Jacqueline said, extending her hand warmly.

Janelle raised a brow playfully and took her hand. "Oh? All good things, I hope."

"Of course," Jacqueline laughed. "He told me he recently found out that you are his sister. And how he is settling into this new relationship. I am so proud of him. He talks about how driven you are and how you grew up right here. It's been amazing getting to know someone so focused and calm. And let me tell you, he makes a killer breakfast. Veggie Omelet and French toast with fresh strawberries this morning!"

Janelle blinked. "Breakfast?" she said under her breath, almost inaudibly. She never knew Julien to scramble an egg, much less whip up an omelet. She exchanged a glance with Cayenne, who raised an eyebrow, and Eva, who leaned in, her voice low but playful.

"This ain't your business, girl," Eva said.

"And it sure ain't your breakfast," Cayenne added, both chuckling.

Julien, catching the vibe, gave a sheepish shrug. "One time. I cooked once."

Janelle laughed, unable to stop herself. "Well, whatever you did, it must've worked."

"See you at church tomorrow," Jacqueline said, grabbing her keys and heading to the car. Julien gave Janelle a nervous smile before leaving to join his new interest.

Janelle's smile faded into disbelief. "Church?" she whispered. "I'm pretty sure the last time Julien was in church was Dad's funeral," she muttered, still smiling.

Eva nudged her. "Girl, stop."

"Yep," Cayenne added. "Zip it!"

Janelle nodded, eyes soft. "I know. I know."

The porch rippled with quiet laughter, the kind that came from deep places, the kind you earned. As the group began to wind down, Olive looked out at the emptying street, the moonlight casting gentle shadows across the grass. Her eyes twinkled as she whispered something low and random. "Lost my favorite pie plate once. Never did find it."

No one said anything for a moment. Then, Red chuckled, and Mildred reached for Olive's hand. Nothing was truly lost as long as someone still came to sit on the porch. And just like that, the porch settled into the night.

The next morning, just after sunrise, Caesar opened the door to the cottage and, once inside, began pacing in front of Janelle's door. She followed him out to find Isaiah sitting on the porch with a drawing pad in his lap.

"Couldn't sleep?" she asked.

Isaiah shook his head and showed her the pad. He had drawn the barn, the cottage, and the porch, all labeled in a child's neat handwriting. "HOME."

Janelle knelt beside him and smiled. "That's beautiful."

Isaiah looked at her. "Do you think Granny Olive will remember everything?"

"I think she'll remember what matters," Janelle said. "And if she forgets, we'll remember for her.

# EPILOGUE

It was quiet on the porch. Summer had nearly folded into fall, and the breeze rustled the last of the oak leaves hanging on above the lane. Cicadas sang. Caesar snored at the foot of the swing, his body twitching to some dream rhythm.

Janelle stepped onto the porch in a soft green and white wrap dress, barefoot, with the bar results letter in one hand and a bottle of cold brew in the other. She'd driven down from Chicago that morning, a single bag in the trunk, her heart beating louder than her playlist. The results were released yesterday. She didn't want to read them alone.

Olive sat on the swing, a blanket tucked over her lap despite the warm breeze. She looked out at the Angel Oak, as if it were telling her stories, some she remembered, and others danced just outside her reach.

"Mama?" Janelle said softly.

Olive turned slowly, her face creasing into a smile. "Did you know your daddy once tried to make a kite out of newspaper and broomsticks? Didn't fly worth a thing, but he swore it was just the wind's fault."

Janelle smiled, taking a seat beside her. "Sounds like him." She held up the envelope, then paused. "I got my bar results."

Olive looked at her, eyes clear for a moment. "Well? What

did they say?"

Janelle exhaled and unsealed the envelope. "I passed."

There was a flicker, a flash of pride, recognition, maybe joy. Then Olive's gaze drifted toward the street again. "Good," she said. "Your daddy would be pleased. "A pause. Then, almost whispering, she added, "Are we waiting on Justice to come in from the barn? He's been gone a while."

Janelle's throat tightened, but she took her mother's hand. "No, Mama. It's just us now."

Olive nodded. "Well, then. Let's sit a while."

They rocked gently in the swing, the creaking wood keeping rhythm with the cicadas' song. Fragmented memories floated between them like fireflies. And from her seat on the porch, Janelle finally felt it. She had come full circle. Truth had bent and broken and reshaped her. But it hadn't undone her. It had led her home.

The screen door creaked, and Marcus stepped onto the porch, holding a bundle of mail. "Just dropped off. You got something from overseas." He handed Janelle the envelope, postmarked from Seoul.

Her eyes caught the return address. U.S. Department of State, Republic of Korea. The recipient. Justice Goodman. The swing slowed. Janelle stared at the envelope, her fingers hovering just above the seal. "What business do you still have in Korea, Daddy?" She whispered.

And the porch, a silent sentinel, bore witness to it all.

# ACKNOWLEDGMENTS

This story was conceived ten years ago, drawing on memories of my childhood in Dayton, Ohio, people who made an impression on my young mind, and later, the feeling of unfinished business after my father passed away unexpectedly. Throughout the healing process, I imagined certain things differently, and intriguing characters began to appear and take shape in my mind. Then came a setting, a plot, and finally, a story.

Over the years, this reimagination has come and gone, interrupted by work, school, and family obligations. As the storyline intensified in my imagination, the characters began to take on lives of their own. Today, I transition from a professional career to a creative one; I am committed to storytelling to inform and transform. As a full-time caregiver for my mother, I often find moments to sit, reflect, and write, resulting in themes that aim to uplift and heal generations.

First and foremost, I would like to acknowledge my father, uncles, and Montgomery County neighbors, who would spend countless hours sitting on the porch, sharing stories.

Thank you, Kim Shur, for your editorial wisdom, which has supported me from the beginning of my serious writing pursuits. Your insight and encouragement have significantly refined this narrative.

Thank you to my early readers, Cheri Reese, Joann Pederi, Kathy Scott, and Nancy Simuel, whose honest feedback shaped this work.

Thank you, Mother, whom I had to remind that this is a work of fiction. Your memory sometimes failed to recall details about our life in Dayton, yet you provided me with nuggets I could embellish to create as I went along. Your love and quiet wisdom planted seeds in me that, over time, blossomed into this story.

Thank you to my family and friends for believing in me.

I want to thank the many eccentric individuals I encountered in Dayton; their stories, quirks, and quiet strength inspired the characters that inhabit this work, breathing life into a fictional world grounded in real humanity.

I am profoundly grateful to my husband, whose extraordinary gifts as a musician and artist infused my writing space with a beautiful balance of rhythm and harmony. Myron, your unwavering guidance and boundless creative spirit not only inspired my writing but also helped breathe life into this story. Thank you for your tender encouragement that gently nudged me to keep writing, even during moments when I felt like abandoning the project. Thank you for composing such a beautiful piece of music to accompany this story. God has blessed me with a gift: the opportunity to create with you.

Readers can listen to the original music for Quiet on the Porch by Myron Lee on msjocelylee.com and other streaming platforms.

# ABOUT THE AUTHOR

Jocelyn Michelle Lee is an author and literary voice for healing, empowerment, and transformation. With a rich history as a growth mindset coach, business leader, and educator, Jocelyn now writes stories and reflections that stir the soul, challenge the status quo, and inspire meaningful change. Her words are rooted in lived experience and a deep belief in the power of storytelling to move people toward peace, freedom, and joy.

With more than 30 years in corporate leadership, consultative sales, and business development, combined with a passion for community service and education, Jocelyn brings a multidimensional perspective to every page she writes.

A National African American Women's Leadership Institute (NAAWLI) fellow, former non-profit board member, and speaker, she has championed financial literacy, mentored rising leaders, and taught at the collegiate level.

Her academic path includes a B.S. in Business Management and M.A. in Religious Studies from Cardinal Stritch University, an M.A. in English from Grand Canyon University, and a Doctorate in Management and Organizational Leadership from the University of Phoenix. Her dissertation focused on mentoring and the advancement of African American women in corporate leadership.

Today, Jocelyn resides in Arizona with Myron, her husband of 43 years, her beloved mother, and Solomon, their faithful Labrador Retriever. Their two sons live nearby, while their daughter lives abroad in Spain.

Through her books and blogs, Jocelyn continues to do what she's always done best, hold space for growth, share wisdom with grace, and invite others to become the best version of themselves.

# QUIET ON THE PORCH TOPICS FOR DISCUSSION

## FAMILY, LEGACY & IDENTITY

1. What does the porch symbolize throughout the novel?

How does its role shift from chapter to chapter, and what does it mean to different characters?

2. How do the concepts of legacy and inheritance, emotional, familial, and material, shape Justice, Olive, and eventually Janelle?

3. What makes a family in this story?

How does the novel challenge or reaffirm traditional definitions of family?

## TRUTH, SECRETS & FORGIVENESS

4. How does the novel explore the tension between protection and secrecy?

Did Olive make the right choice in how and when she revealed the truth to Janelle?

5. Several characters carry secrets.

Which ones do you think were necessary, and which were damaging? Why?

6. How is forgiveness portrayed in the novel?

What does it cost the characters to extend or accept it?

## TRAUMA & RESILIENCE

7. The novel shows how people carry both trauma and healing across generations.

In what ways do the characters repeat or break cycles?

8. Justice builds things to cope. Olive returns to order. Eva sings.

How do different characters respond to grief or guilt?

## LOVE IN MANY FORMS

9. Romantic love, parental love, chosen love, and broken love all live in these pages.

Which relationship moved you the most, and why?

10. What does Janelle and Julien's relationship reveal about identity, choice, and love's complexity?

Did their ending feel hopeful to you?

## STRUCTURE & CRAFT

11. How did the novel's use of real-time scenes from the past (rather than traditional flashbacks) affect your reading experience?

12. The POV shifts, especially the Porch's voice, add layers to the storytelling.

Did the omniscient narrator feel trustworthy or poetic to you? What did it reveal that no one else could?

## COMMUNITY & SETTING

13. Oakwood is more than a backdrop, it's a character.

How does the township shape the events of the story?

14. How does the novel explore the impact of public opinion and community storytelling (e.g., Penny, the porch banter, the church)?

## FINAL REFLECTION

15. If you could ask any character one question, who would it be and what would you ask?

16. What moment lingered with you the most after finishing the book? Why?

# NOTES:

# NOTES:

# NOTES:

# NOTES: